Copyright

This book is a work of fiction. Names, characters, businesses, organizations, places, events, and incidents are either an idea from the author's personal creativity or used fictitiously. Any resemblance to actual places, persons, events, or locales is completely coincidental.

Trigger Warnings:
Alcohol, sex, graphic sex, blood, death, fighting, violence, decapitation, abduction/kidnapping, age gap, drinking, hostages, PTSD, murder, swearing, mention of torture, mention of rape.

Dedication

This book is dedicated to those who struggle with mental health.

Table of Contents

Chapter 1

The smell of garbage fills the air around me as I run on four paws toward Corey, while he struggles to fight back a winged creature. Bloody gouges cover his side where it's gotten him, but it won't hurt him much longer.

Stupid Imp, why don't you pick on someone your own size? I send out my thoughts and it whips its head toward me, letting out a snarl. I try not to panic, as more fly from the trees, but instead push my fear down. With a roar, I launch myself at it, snapping my jaws around its head. With a yank, I rip it off and spit it on the ground.

Corey shakes himself, the wounds already starting to heal along his wolf's coat.

Thanks, Em. Did you bring backup? I found a nest of them.

Yeah, Adam and Zeke were right behind me with a few other Betas.

I snarl at the Imps gathered around us before sending out a pulse of power that pushes them back. It surprises them, causing several to stumble and fall over, but the Imps recover quickly. They know better than to push a hellhound too far.

A group of wolves and two vampires burst through the trees, pulling the Imps' attention away from us momentarily. I keep my eyes on the group as they grab the Imps closest to them, tearing them limb from limb. The wolves move past the vamps and snag the Imps attempting to fly off with their massive jaws. This gives Corey and me time to regroup.

Once he's ready, we launch into the attack ourselves. The Imps scream and screech as our group works through them, tearing them to pieces. As the last Imp is taken out, a light breeze lets me know Zeke is at my side. He rests his hand on my shoulder as I continue to glare at the bodies lying around us.

"You could probably torch them all now, love," he states, patting my side as if I were a puppy.

I shake my fur in response and turn my head to look at him. The Imps have continued to terrorize our pack more since I've been back. I can't help but wonder if it's not one of those triplet generals pushing them on us. I know only one of them was taken down in my escape from Hell.

Okay, I will. Everyone step back so you don't get hit by my flames.

It's convenient you can do that, you know? Seth, one of our packs, lead Betas, says from somewhere in the clearing.

I have to agree. It's made things a lot easier since you've gotten back. Adam huffs from where he stands across the clearing.

I appreciate the support, guys, but let's get this over with. I huff and call my magic up. I plant my paws into the soft earth at my feet and glance around to make sure I won't set any trees on fire. I let my flames loose. The black fire bursts forth from my jaws and eats the Imps' bodies away to black ash that drifts to the earth in seconds. It leaves scorch marks where they once were and thankfully, it's nothing too bad. Grass will one day cover it.

Well, that's done, Corey says cheerily and I huff in response. They act like using my magic is some easy feat. Really, it exhausts me, and my energy reserves are now on E.

I let out a yawn, wishing I could be done with this day, but knowing I can't be.

Yes. Let's head back. Is there anything you guys want me to teach you today?

I turn and feel Zeke stay at my side. His warmth and scent are calming. The others fall in line behind us as we make the trek back to the pack house.

I'm thankful that so far, the Imps have kept to the woods. It's helped us keep it a secret from normal humans. They might think the apocalypse was coming if they saw all these demons. Even I question it sometimes with the amount of them showing up. Corey and Adam swear it wasn't this bad until I got back.

Maybe just a few drills to help the younger ones some more? Your sisters have been showing excellent advancement compared to the others. I may move them up soon, Seth voices. He's taken over training us all more in depth since I got back. He received special permission from Alpha Gale to step off patrol duty to do so. Alpha Gale approved reluctantly. He's been awfully standoffish since I returned. He's also stopped pushing the contract between Adam and me, yet he won't destroy it.

I refuse to acknowledge the contract, and Adam respects my wishes. He also chooses to ignore it. We agree it holds no sway over us anymore. I'm a completely different person after being dragged to Hell against my will and making a narrow escape.

I've only been back a few days, but it seems like forever ago that I was there. I know my days are numbered and I'll have to return soon, but I'm pushing to do all that I can before I go. This pack needs to be strong for the divide that's coming.

Adam has been looking into past records regarding pack occurrences and titles dating back to the time when he was born and his mother's death shortly after. It turns out that Corey's dad was still in training at that time, so he's off the hook for being involved with his mother's sacrifice.

I still find it hard to believe that Alpha Gale sacrificed his mate for power. Who in their right mind does that? Mates are supposed to be a forever thing. It had to have been painful in more ways than one. Losing a mate is like losing half of your soul.

Also, strangely, there were only a handful of Betas close to Alpha Gale at that time. Most of them are dead, but two remain. One is Beta Ralph Ward, who continues to guard the pack house, and another is a male who left the pack shortly after the time of the sacrifice. His name is Onyx Lane, and he lives a couple of states over in Louisiana. The records don't list a town, but we're working to find him. With as much technology in existence today, there has to be some way to track him down.

I'm pleased they're doing so well, but I'm worried my family may be targeted more after my escape, I say, and several growls fill the air. We've kept the bit about me being Lucifer's daughter on the down low as much as possible. We told Seth in hopes that we could trust him with the secret. He's vital in keeping everyone safe and has vowed to do everything he can to teach the pack what it needs, for when the time comes that there will be a massive attack. The vamps, on the other hand, know who I am. With Zeke being their prince, he made them vow to tell no one. They are very loyal to their kingdom.

Half of the pack was on board for the more intense training at all levels. Those who aren't for it were given the option to stick with the lighter schedule in place before. That way, they're still learning what they need to, but they won't be the pack's main attack and defense.

With the new training plans in place, Corey, Zeke, Adam, and I have tried to keep our eye on Alpha Gale, but it's been difficult. He disappears at random times and we're not sure where he goes. Does he know that we're on to what he's done? We still don't understand why he needs so much power or if he is even still communicating with the witch. There are so many things we don't know, but we have to find something to take before the elder council, to get them involved. If we could get an eyewitness account of the sacrifice, that would be the best, but getting one of the two Betas to confess what they saw may be another issue.

You know we will keep them safe, Ember. As future Alpha, I can promise you that. Adam's words are reassuring, but in reality, if a group of higher-level warriors from Hell showed up, this pack wouldn't stand a chance by itself. It's nothing against them, but fighting those trained warriors of Greed's was brutal. Hell, they got strong hits in on an angel and vamp who have been around for ages.

I nod my head to let him know I heard his words but remain quiet. With all the things I have to worry about right now, I need to do my best to focus. *Seth, have you been writing down some of the training plans I shared?* I ask, ignoring the headache forming.

Yep, I'm making quite the nice little booklet. Your angel friends sure know their stuff, Seth says as he trots up beside me. His dark fur is all ruffled still from the fight.

Okay, I want to look those over again tonight and add some things. I want to make sure we have as much down as we can. It'll be helpful.

Whatever you say. I'll send it over with Adam tonight, he responds and I roll my eyes. The pack still thinks we're going to be their Alpha and Luna. Adam hasn't exactly started looking for another Luna, so we've just let them think what they will. Most also don't realize that Zeke is my mate. The ruse has helped keep a level of civility with many of the pack, and we don't want to upset that balance before we have to. Outing our Alpha will cause enough problems when it happens.

Great, okay, I'm going to run ahead and stop by the house. I'll meet you all at the pack house for some more training. I shake my fur and take off, not giving anyone a chance to say anything else. Zeke stays at my side and I'm thankful for that. It gives me time to let my guard down. Once we're near the house, I shift back from my giant black fiery wolf to my human body.

I let a deep sigh escape my lips as I turn and lean into Zeke's open arms. He folds them around me and I let my emotions go. Tears stream down my face as everything presses down on me. Ulric's loss weighs on me heavily. I still don't know if he's dead or alive because I can't feel anything in the bond. I hate it, and it makes me assume the worst even though I'm fighting the thought tooth and nail.

"Let it all out, love. I've got you. I don't know why you hold it in like you do," Zeke says as he rubs circles on my back.

I sob for a few minutes before pulling it together enough to respond. "I have to be strong. You know we've only shared bits and pieces with everyone. I don't want anyone to threaten Adam's position if all the secrets get out. You know they will eventually. Once Kai shows up to take me back, word will be all over town about who my real father is."

"Then we'll deal with that when the time comes. Trust those you care about with everything, though. We will need them when shit hits the fan. We need to all be united. No secrets. Isn't that what's caused issues with this pack to begin with?"

I wipe at the tears still leaking from my eyes. "I guess so. Ugh. It's all just so heavy. How am I supposed to do this?"

"One step at a time, love. Now, what are you needing from the house?" Zeke steps back and looks down at me. He still towers over me. You would think that my human body would have gotten some height from my powers being unleashed, but nope.

I shrug. "I wanted to make sure my sisters were going to come to training and check on my parents. I want to use every free moment I have to see them. I missed them when I was stuck in Greed's castle."

"Okay, well, let's see if they're here." He turns me gently and holds my hand as we make our way toward my parents' front porch.

Since I've been gone, they gave it a touchup with fresh white paint and new flowers. There are even new boards in place where a few had rotted, making the entire porch look almost brand new. It needed a lot of work. I guess it gave my dad something to focus on while I was gone.

We make our way up the steps and enter the house. The smell of fried chicken fills the entryway and we follow it to the kitchen, where both my parents are making lunch.

"Oh hey, hon, did you guys take that group down?" my dad asks as he stands over the stove.

"Yeah, it was a large group. I was shocked at how many there were. Things could easily have gone south had we not arrived on time," I respond and pull Zeke toward the table where my mom sits, sipping on a glass of sweet tea.

She stands quickly and pulls me into a hug. "Oh, sweetheart, I hate that you have to fight them. Is Corey okay, then?"

I pull out of her hug with a groan. "Mom, I'm the strongest wolf in the pack now. I can handle myself. He's good. He was super lucky, and they only got a few gouges in on him."

"Just because you're the strongest doesn't mean I like you fighting. Zeke, you took care of her?" My mom turns to my mate and I roll my eyes.

"You know I did, Kyra. I always do, even when she doesn't need it. Did Tansy and Winnie go to the pack house already?" Zeke asks, changing the topic at hand.

"They did. I sent chicken with them. They left about an hour ago," my dad says loudly as he pulls a large piece of chicken from the frying pan. My stomach growls in response.

"It sounds like you need to eat, love. I swear your appetite has doubled since you were gone. You eat more than any wolf in this pack." My mom pulls me toward the table and pushes me into a chair before spinning around and going to the cabinet.

I watch her as she busies herself, making me and Zeke glasses of tea. "I mean, I did come into my powers and it does use a lot of energy when I use them, so I can see how my appetite would increase."

"Are you getting snarky?" My mom pauses and turns around with a glare.

I shake my head. "No, Mom, just stating a fact. So, are Tansy and Winnie enjoying their training? Seth spoke highly of them today."

"They are!" my dad exclaims and turns from the stove. "That's all they talk about anymore. I love it. I want my girls to be the strongest they can be. They really look up to you."

"I'm glad they enjoy it. I want them to know how to take care of themselves. Maybe they'll develop some powers of their own? I know most of the time that it stays in the Alpha's bloodline, but occasionally it shows up elsewhere." I smile as my mom sets a plate of food in front of me and two glasses in front of Zeke. One is filled with blood and the other sweet tea.

"It's a possibility," my dad says as he takes a seat with his own plate. "My grandfather was an Alpha of this pack once upon a time. He was challenged by Alpha Gale's father and was defeated."

"What? I thought the Courser family has always been the Alpha line." I gape at my dad.

"No, that only happened a few decades ago. They don't like it to be known, especially since the pack has grown so much over the years. It's strange really."

I turn back to my food as my dad goes silent, and I contemplate the information he just shared with me. It would be amazing if my sisters developed something. Then I would feel a little better about not being around all the time. I have nightmares about them being taken like those shifters I helped rescue were. I don't want them to go through what they did.

So many of the girls have struggled to adapt to life here again. They spook easily, but I've made sure they get everything they need and that a few of the males in the pack have kept a watchful eye on them to keep them safe. Some of them have even found their true mate since returning.

"Well, I guess we'll have to wait and see. Things are changing around here again," I finally say and dig into my food. I'll need the boost for training.

Chapter 2

Zeke and I take our time walking to the pack house, our bellies full of fried chicken and potatoes. My parents have always done a fantastic job when cooking a meal. I've always thought more of the pack would like to hang out at our house because of the food, but thankfully, that's never been a thing. It lets us have a bit more peace. I've always wondered if it was because of the contract that they kept their distance, but maybe not?

The sound of fighting meets our ears as we walk hand-in-hand. Seth has already started the training, which is good. They need all they can get. I don't know how much time I have until Kai shows up to drag me back to Hell.

I smile and look over at Zeke, who returns it. "It makes you happy to know they're working hard, huh?" he asks.

"Yes. I know they'll be prepared when the time comes." I turn my attention ahead of me and we make our way around the large white house.

The pack house has a huge porch, and the flower beds are always kept neat and tidy. It has many rooms and conference rooms for pack business and members. Most Betas stay at the pack house, but many have chosen to have their own home with their mates.

Growing up in the pack house was rough for Adam. His father has always been on his case about training and staying on top of pack business.

I always thought it was a little obsessive honestly, but I'm starting to see things in a different light.

We edge around the house to the training area, which is set up behind it. Since I returned, we've made new practice dummies to mimic several types of demons and those akin to what I practiced on in Hell. They're more durable than what we used previously and do better against my flames.

My heart soars as I see Seth working with my twin sisters. He has them double-teaming him and deflects their moves, but it appears that they've gotten a few hits on him. A bruise is forming on his left cheek. I instantly feel joyful and proud to know they're kicking ass.

I walk over to the three and pause a short distance away to avoid getting hit. "Well, it looks like you two are the stars of the show," I say and they stop and turn to face me with grins on their faces. Seth smiles and steps back, trying to catch his breath.

My sisters rush to me and pull me into a hug as Winnie says, "Oh, Em, I'm so excited! Seth says we're moving up to work with stronger opponents!"

Tansy pulls away from the hug. "We're both excited. I got past Seth's block and nailed him in the face. See his bruise." She giggles.

I laugh as Seth saunters up and rolls his eyes. "It was a lucky shot. Don't get a big head. I'll be ready next time."

Tansy turns to him and sticks out her tongue. "Sure you will. We'll see." Turning back to me, she asks, "So, Em, are you going to show us some new moves?"

"Yes, but then I need to go over some things with Seth regarding new training schedules." I meet Seth's questioning gaze and he shrugs.

"That's fine with me. Do you need someone to help you with the demonstration?" he asks.

"Actually, watching you with my sisters has given me an idea. It would be good to teach the younger ones how to handle more than one opponent. Gather everyone up and then meet Zeke and me on the platform at the back of the training area. Both of you have different levels of speed and moves, so it'll be fun." I turn and smile at Zeke.

"You think you can best us both?" Zeke smirks.

"We'll get her, Zeke, don't you worry." Seth pats his shoulder before turning away.

"Yeah, you go ahead and think that, Seth," I say loudly as he moves away from us. I grab Zeke by the hand now that my sisters have let me out of the hug. They follow Zeke and me to the back of the training area, and I hop on the training platform, shaking with anticipation.

Zeke follows suit and walks to the other end as we wait on Seth. Several groups of trainees move in to watch with curious expressions on their faces. They're excited to see what we've got, but I know they won't be as excited once they start practicing it.

Once Seth is in position, I turn to face the crowd. I spot Corey and Adam at the back. I wonder if they placed a bet on who would go down first. I'd be surprised if they didn't.

"Alright, everyone. I know some of you know how to take on an attack by more than one opponent, but we're going to change it up. Each of you will work against one vampire and one shifter at the same time. You'll need to maintain your focus and use all your senses. Each attack will be different. Pay close attention to how the three of us move. We'll spar for a couple of minutes, then have you break off into groups. You may have to rotate, depending on the size of each group, but you'll each work on this for the rest of the afternoon. As you know, we have more than just shifters and vamps to deal with these days." I nod at the crowd and turn back to face Seth and Zeke.

Each of them is on opposite sides of the sparring mat and has a calculated expression on their faces. I wink at Zeke, and they take that as a cue to start. They move toward me, almost in sync. I laugh and spin like a ballerina out of their path. They quickly turn themselves and smile.

I move in and the two converge on me. I force my magic to stay within as I dodge, punch, parry, and cartwheel to avoid getting hit. They have similar moves, but I get a few punches in on them. Seth and Zeke both land punches to my ribs, but they are light, having barely hit their mark. I'm slightly faster than they are.

We continue to practice like this for a solid twenty minutes before calling it quits. Each of us is sweating and panting with fatigue.

"Great work, guys!" I smile and rest my hands on my knees.

Seth smiles and turns to the crowd. "Alright, remember what she said. Get to work!"

Zeke sits on the mat and motions for me to sit next to him. "You did awesome, dear. I don't know why you're sweating so much though."

I plop down next to him and lightly punch his shoulder. "I had to stay on my toes with you guys. That wasn't as easy as I thought it would be. You two are much faster than I realized."

Seth sits next to me with a spiral-bound notebook in hand. "I didn't exactly hold back, Ember. You're one tough cookie."

I laugh. "I guess that's a compliment, right? Oh, here, let me see what you've got written down so far." I reach for the notebook and Seth passes it over.

"I can't help but wonder why you're pushing so hard to get all this stuff done so quickly. Is there something I'm missing here? I mean, you mentioned that bit about your father, but I still feel like there's something else."

Adam and Corey walk up at that moment, and I watch Seth as he stares at me. It's like he's willing me to let him in.

"I think we should move into one of the conference rooms if we're going to discuss this. I think we should fill him in, Ember," Adam says.

I tilt my head and look at Seth. "If we give you more information, it means you're willingly siding with us with what's coming."

"That sounds like trouble. What is coming exactly?" Seth asks, and I push up from the ground.

"Come on. Let's get you filled in. We need another eye on some things anyway." I turn toward the house and follow Adam as we walk through the back door and down to one of the conference rooms. Corey checks the other rooms to make sure they're vacant, and he and Zeke check the room to make sure there aren't any cameras or mics. We don't want to let this information out.

"You guys are acting strange about this. What's so big that you need to check the place to see if it's bugged?" Seth asks as he takes a chair at the long wooden table.

I slide into one across from him, and Zeke rests against the wall behind me. I roll my eyes, trying to decide whether it's a territorial thing or a protective one. Corey stands by the door while Adam moves in next to Seth.

"Okay, so we told you my dad was Lucifer, but what we left out was that I'm on borrowed time before I have to go back to Hell. Kai, a hellhound who helped us escape from Greed's castle, is his top general and is informing Lucifer of my existence. We're trying to figure out a way to report Alpha Gale to the elder's council for sacrificing Starla, Adam's mom, as well." I pause and watch Seth as my words sink in.

"Do what now? He sacrificed her? How do you know this?" he asks, completely ignoring the first half of my words.

I sigh and rub my forehead. "My informant was Zendaya. Apparently, the witch has worked with Greed some and she's the same one who gave Alpha Gale the power from the sacrifice. I don't know many details, just that he had a Beta help him with whatever kind of ritual they did. We need to find proof or someone to completely share their version of what happened so Adam can take over and properly lead the pack before corruption gets worse. That also may be part of why we've had such an increase in attacks other than the fact that I upset a lot of people by existing."

"Holy fucking shit. You're serious about this. Fuck. What about the part you said you're on borrowed time? Are they planning to kidnap you?" Seth growls.

"No, I'll have to go willingly. I'm part of a bigger plan, apparently. Don't ask for details on that because I don't have much there either. We could use your help to try to put together something on Alpha Gale, though." I nod over at Adam, who takes up the next part.

Adam nods in return before turning to look at Seth. "I've been doing some research in the books, trying to figure out which Betas were working with my father around the time of my mother's death. Not many of them are still alive. I don't know if he had them killed off or what, but one left the pack to live in another state and the other remains here. Beta Ward may have been in on it. He's the one who remains. The other is Onyx Lane. We think one of them may know something about what happened."

Seth looks between Adam and me. "How exactly do you plan to get information from either of them on this subject?"

Adam shrugs as he says, "We're not sure exactly, but I think we should try Onyx Lane first. Were you ever close to him? If we make it a day trip, maybe it won't look so suspicious."

Seth looks at him with a serious expression. "If we're going to leave pack land, we're going to have to be sneaky. Your father is still restricting many of the higher ups from leaving. You and Ember are still on that list, despite new circumstances. No offense, Zeke." Seth turns and nods at Zeke.

"None taken. You're obviously with us on things, so what's the plan?" Zeke smiles.

Corey speaks up from his place at the door. "I think we should convince Alpha Gale that Seth is taking us on a special practice run and use that as our cover to travel out to find Onyx. Simple."

I frown. "Is that too simple, though?"

"Actually, that's a great idea. Onyx did train me for a bit, so I'm sure I can find his number somewhere. I may still have it on my phone." Seth pulls out his phone and begins scrolling through his contacts.

"Great, while you're looking, hand me that notebook and I'll jot down some training ideas. How soon do you think we can get our plan in motion?" I ask as Seth slides the notebook across the table.

He looks down at his phone again. "Assuming this is still the same number, I think we can get it together and move out tomorrow, especially since we don't know when your new buddy will show up to retrieve you. Ah, here it is. I'll text him. Do you guys want to go back out to train some more or call it a day?" Seth looks at the guys.

"After I jot this stuff down, I'll be back out there. Let's meet on the training mat in the morning to discuss if you heard back from Onyx. Then we'll go from there." I smile and everyone nods in agreement. I watch momentarily as they all file out. Zeke winks at me as he goes, and I spend the next hour and a half writing down training formations before joining them.

Chapter 3

After a short run the following morning, I sit in the middle of one of the sparring mats as I stretch, waiting for the rest of our small group to arrive. I hope Seth figured something out to tell Alpha Gale and that we're able to sneak away with no issues. I also hope Alpha Gale hasn't picked up on any of our suspicions.

I turn my gaze and watch Adam and Corey exit the pack house with somber expressions. Seth follows behind them and they shuffle their feet slightly. Zeke has yet to arrive, so I continue stretching as they move closer.

"Why do you guys look so grim?" I ask as they drop to the mat to join me on my stretches.

Adam meets my gaze. "Well, we just got our asses chewed by my dad. On the bright side, we're clear to go on this training trip." He lifts his hands and air quotes his words for emphasis.

Corey adds in, "The bad side is, we must come up with something to tell him as a report on how we do against whatever opponent we face. He doesn't want a repeat of Alaska."

Seth shrugs. "I tried to convince him that it wouldn't be a replay, but he has his suspicions since you and Zeke are going. He thinks you two are going to run off together."

I roll my eyes. "Why is he worried about that? I could leave any time I want. His power has no influence over me. I could break my parents out if needed as well."

Adam scratches his chin before speaking. "I think he wants to keep your power within the pack because it makes us all stronger in his eyes. I don't think it's possible for you to share your power with us, so it's a crazy idea."

Corey shrugs. "It fits."

"It does, and it seems he's moving his plans ahead while keeping others distracted. Did you know he launched an attack on a neighboring pack last night? He forced the Pine Pack in western Oklahoma to yield and be absorbed by our pack. He isn't going to tell anyone just yet until he has an excuse. Apparently, some of the older Betas have been helping him on his personal agenda." Zeke surprises us as he plops down next to us.

Adam's mouth hangs open momentarily before he asks, "How did you find this out?"

Zeke smiles mischievously. "I followed him, of course. I don't need that much sleep. I only rest for one reason these days." He winks at me, and I blush.

"Okay, so you followed him? Did he do any of the attacking? I'm slightly offended that I wasn't included. How did you avoid detection?" Seth asks pointedly, looking at Zeke.

Zeke sighs before turning his gaze from me to Seth. "I followed in the shadows and stayed in the top of the trees. He let the Betas do the work. They all had a grey glow about them during the attack. I don't know if he's given them something or if the witch is helping, but it's not good."

I scratch my head. "Do you think there's a way to video one of the attacks? With an eyewitness and video proof, we could easily get the council on top of this."

Corey frowns. "It may be too dangerous to do that, but you make a good point. What if he's more powerful than the elder council? Have any of you thought of that?"

We all pause, letting his words sink in. Could he be?

Adam grunts. "I guess we'll just have to wait and see. Maybe we need to make some sneaky pack connections and prepare in case it does come to something that the council needs help with. I don't want to see a massive war, but if that's what it takes, then we need to be prepared."

"Fuck," Seth groans and we all nod in agreement.

"I may be able to get some other allies on our side. It depends on how soon things fall into place with this and when Ember has to return." Zeke's words get quieter as he speaks.

"Stupid family issues," I mumble. "Well, how soon can we leave? Did you get in touch with Onyx?"

Seth sits up straight and pulls his cell out of his pocket. "I did. He said we could stop by. I didn't tell him what it was about, just that I have some newbies looking to learn information about what it's like switching packs. I told him it was for a school project. He may be shocked when we all show up, but we'll make it work."

"Great, so he may slam the door in our faces when we arrive?" I ask sullenly.

"Eh, we'll see. Now, do you all want to practice before we go?" Seth looks at us as we finish stretching.

"I mean, I ran this morning so I'm good." I shrug.

Adam tilts his head to the side. "I think we could use some downtime. Let's go."

Corey pushes into standing. "Whose vehicle are we taking?"

We all stand, and Seth suggests, "I think we should take one of the pack's SUVs. It'll hold all of us. I'll drive."

We follow Seth across the training area toward the detached garage on the other side of the house. It's where all the packs' extra vehicles are kept and any larger training items. Its exterior is white to match the main house but as we enter, it makes you feel like you're walking into a cave.

The large room is all black and dim lights. Even the concrete floor is stained dark. It makes the stainless-steel drawers and cars almost pop out against the darkness. It's kind of trippy at first, but as my eyes adjust, everything seems to settle down.

Seth leads us to a large white SUV, and we climb in. I squeeze my way into the back bench seat with Zeke hot on my tail. Corey takes the middle seat and Adam and Seth sit in the front.

Hitting a button near the visor, the large door at the front of the garage opens, letting natural light spill in. He maneuvers us easily out of the darkness, and we head down the drive.

"How long do you think it'll take to get to Onyx's location?" I ask with a yawn.

Seth meets my gaze in the rearview mirror briefly before looking back to the road. "We should be there in about three hours, give or take a few minutes. We'll stop halfway there for some food and to use the restrooms."

"Sounds great. I think I'm going to nap. Wake me when we get there," I say and lean over on Zeke, who wraps his arms around me.

"Will do, boss," Adam says sarcastically from the front seat, and I lift my arm to flip him the bird, keeping my eyes closed.

The men in the car laugh and I smile. Zeke rubs circles on my back and I feel myself drift. I think I've been pushing myself too hard these last few days since I've been back, but I need everyone prepared for what's coming.

§

A few hours later, we turn off onto a small road leading into a quaint little neighborhood. The houses are all cookie cutter and match one another with the only distinction being the flower beds. They're cute but the biggest thing about the neighborhood is the bayou that runs behind them.

From the road you can see that it's wide and on the opposite side of where the houses are, there are tons of trees. Tall grass grows at their base and it's perfect to hide a shifter in. It makes me curious as to how many houses on this street belong to shifters.

We pull up in front of a house with a flower bed filled with blooming blue plants. Its windows are decked out in white trim and the front door is painted a light shade of blue like the flowers. The colors give me a brief sense of calm, but my nerves linger, and butterflies continue to dance in my belly.

"So, this is where he lives?" I ask, meeting Seth's gaze as he parks the SUV.

"Yes, this is the address he gave me." He pushes his door open. "Okay everyone out."

The guys groan and we all file out. Seth leads us to the door, and knocks. We all listen intently to heavy footsteps growing closer to us from inside the house.

The door opens a moment later to reveal a tall male with black hair, grey eyes, and an athletic build. He takes us in before meeting Seth's gaze. A massive smile breaks out across his face and his entire being changes to remind me of a giant teddy bear.

"Wow, Seth, it's been ages, buddy! How ya been? Are these the young'ins you mentioned? Y'all come on in!" He steps aside and motions us in.

The guys follow Seth in and Zeke hovers behind me. I'm sandwiched between him and Adam. The door closes behind us and we all turn to meet Onyx's gaze unsure of where to go.

"I'm Onyx if you all didn't know that already. We can head into my living room just down the hall there. Anyone want something to drink? I've got fresh sweet tea my mate made in the fridge. She'll be home later." He looks us all over.

"Tea would be wonderful, buddy. I didn't know you found your mate. When did that happen?" Seth responds, carrying the conversation for us.

"Oh, it's quite a story but I'll save it for another time. We've been together for about four years now." Onyx shrugs.

"That's wonderful man." Seth pats Onyx on the shoulder and he beams.

"So down this hall is the living room?" I ask, pulling their attention to me.

"Yes, right that way. I'll grab the tea," Onyx says and darts off toward the kitchen.

I turn and the rest of the group walks with me into a large room filled with an enormous leather sectional. It's dark charcoal with light blue throw pillows. It matches the black-and-blue decorations placed tastefully around the room. A large television hangs above a fireplace on one wall and large windows are on another. In the middle of the room before the sectional is a coffee table with a vase filled with flowers which are of course blue. I can't help but wonder which member of the household loves this color, Onyx, or his mate?

We sit down around the coffee table to wait for Onyx to return. Only a minute seems to go by before he comes down the hall with a tray filled with glasses, a pitcher of tea, and a plate of cookies. My eyes widen as I see the cookies and both Zeke and Corey throw me knowing glances. I stick my tongue out at them and as soon as the tray is on the table, I grab two.

Chuckling, Onyx asks, "Hungry, are you?"

Corey and Zeke snicker as I nod but I mind my manners and wait to speak until I've swallowed my bit of cookie. "Yes. These are delicious! Did you make these?"

The rest of the group reaches for one and I grab a glass of tea as Onyx responds, "I did. It's my great-grandmother's old recipe. I'll give you a copy of it if you'd like."

"I would love that. One can never have too many cookie recipes." I catch Seth rolling his eyes at my words.

"I guess I better introduce everyone, Onyx. I'm sorry I didn't do so immediately." Seth shrugs and points to Corey first. "This is Corey, he's the next main Beta. The future Alpha here is Adam. This young lady is Ember and her mate Zeke."

"Wait, you're mated to a vampire? How does that work? No offense, of course," Onyx asks, looking between Zeke and me.

I tense and look at Zeke before responding. "It's a long story. Maybe best told at another time. Thank you for having us today."

Onyx quirks his brow and sets his glass of tea down. "So, you guys had some questions for me regarding changing packs?" He seems concerned and I feel tension ripple between us all.

"Well, yes, they do want to learn about that, but they also have some other questions too." Seth relaxes back onto the couch, holding his tea close. I guess that means one of us should take the lead.

I look at Adam and he shrugs before turning his gaze to Onyx. "Well, really, we wanted to know why you left. Did you see something that made you want to leave?"

Onyx looks at Adam warily. "I felt called to another pack. That's part of how I met my mate. Why?"

I stare at the ceiling, hoping shit doesn't hit the fan with this topic. Is there a way to gently prod what we need out of him? Frustration boils in my blood as I take a few breaths.

Adam takes a moment before responding. "We were just curious. There is an event that's come to my attention recently about my father that concerns me. I want to correct the mistakes he's made in my pack."

Onyx glares and then turns to Seth with a scowl. "What is this really about, Seth? Did you all come to interrogate me?"

I can no longer just sit, so I speak up, "We did not come to interrogate. Alpha Gale sacrificed his wife for power, and we need proof to kick his ass out of the pack and fix shit. Care to fill us in on if you were there?" I feel heat rise in my body and I know that my eyes may be glowing. I feel hot and Zeke rests a hand on my shoulder, pulling me back to reality.

Onyx looks at me and then to Adam. "Are you sure you two aren't supposed to be mated? She seems to have a lot of power."

"Would you fucking answer the question," I say, remaining seated. Everyone flinches. I'm too tired to beat around the bush. This problem needs to be fixed before more get hurt.

"What is in it for me if I help you? Won't he just send his little group of devoted Betas after me?" Onyx sneers and I feel my blood boil.

"Look, we're trying to clean out those he corrupted. He's trying to take over neighboring packs now and we want to stop him. I want to form alliances with neighboring packs, not rule. We can help keep you, your mate, and your pack safe if you'll help us," Adam buts in and I'm thankful because my fuse is getting shorter. I just want to get answers and get things moving.

"I guess that would be fair but how do I know he won't find a way around your help? He's a crafty bastard. That's why there are only two of us who remember what happened." Onyx looks down at his lap and I notice that his hands are trembling.

My anger dissipates a little. "So, you do know what happened?"

He meets my gaze. "Yes. I'll never forget that horrible night."

I go to ask what happened when we hear the door open, and slam shut. Footsteps are heard moving down the hall quickly as a voice filled with fear asks, "Onyx, where are you?"

A curvy woman with long blond hair and blue eyes enters the room, and she looks at us all. I notice an odd aura about her before she asks, "What the hell is going on? Why do we have two creatures from Hell and random shifters in our living room? Oh, and a fucking group of demons and a savage-looking angel outside?"

A chorus of "what" resounds through the room, and I jump to my feet. Onyx barrels across the room and steps before his mate, glaring at me. "What the fuck does she mean by two creatures of Hell? I see just the vampire."

The woman looks around Onyx at me. "Love, she's a hellhound. What is going on?"

"Look, we can explain later. I need you to tell me what the angel outside looks like." I rush my words and feel Zeke and Corey hovering behind me.

The woman looks at me and tilts her head. "I'm Juniper. The angel outside has black cropped hair and black wings. He has a group of demons surrounding the house. I wasn't sure what to do and ran into the house after pulling into the drive. I've never been taught any magic strong enough to take them on. I'm part witch but I don't have much training with that part of my blood."

I gape at her and look over my shoulder at Zeke. "Fuck. Is it one of the triplets?"

"Who are the triplets again?" Corey asks and Adam's gaze swings to mine.

"Wait. As in one of the ones who almost killed you?" Adam's words are quiet.

Seth growls, "Do we need to take them out?"

I turn back to Onyx and Juniper who watch us curiously. "Would you guys care to join us in a fight? I promise to fill you in on what they're doing here after. We're going to need some extra help."

Onyx looks at Juniper and then turns back to me. "We'll help however we can. I do have to call this into the pack though. They may come join us. I'm not sure how they got past some of them to get here, honestly."

I let out a sigh. "Thanks, I appreciate it. Let's go see who this is and if we can't de-escalate things. Maybe there won't be a fight?"

Zeke scoffs over my shoulder. "I doubt it, love."

I roll my eyes and we follow Onyx down the hall. Juniper stays close to me as we walk, glancing at me curiously. I try to ignore her glances but it's weird.

Filing out the door, I frown at the number of Imps, blue-skinned demons, and green-skinned ones, standing between us and the angel. I meet his gaze and cringe as I realize it's Magi.

Taking a deep breath and letting it out, I steady myself as I ask, "How did you find me, Magi?"

He laughs. "I've had demons tracking you since I woke up. How dare you steal what is mine? I let Prospero off the hook after realizing he'd been duped too, but I've come to reclaim my prize and my unborn child. Where is she?"

I cross my arms and step in front of Onyx, who was still in front of me, and let my wings unfurl. I hear Juniper gasp loudly and feel the energy change as Corey, Adam, and Seth shift. I register a delayed energy change as Onyx and Juniper shift as well and we stand facing the group before us.

"You'll never have her back. I hate that you've come all this way just to get your ass kicked again." I smirk and ready myself to attack.

He laughs. "I beg to differ. I almost beat you before. I'm a seasoned fighter unlike your group of stinky dogs."

The wolves growl behind me and I quirk my head to the side. "You know, you're right that you're a seasoned fighter, but I think we can take you." I smile and let myself change from my angel-winged self to my hellhound.

I growl as I sink my claws into the earth and Magi smirks in response. Before we move to attack, I let out a torrent of black flames that circles the demons and pushes them together. Magi steps back out of reach and stands behind the line of fire. It frustrates me that he isn't stuck in the circle, but I launch forward and unleash myself on his group. The wolves follow suit, and growls, squeals, and screams fill the air.

Before long, we have most of the demons taken down and I glance up to notice a group of wolves surrounding us. Magi looks uncomfortable as he watches them, but none of them move. I recall my fire and the remaining demons attempt to flee, only to be cut down by the large group around us. With them taken care of, I turn my focus to Magi.

I shift back to my body and let my wings remain visible as I speak. "Are you ready for this?" I approach him and gently pull the long sword, given to me the night of the ball, from my back where I keep it hidden all the time now.

He smiles and, in a blink, propels himself toward me wordlessly. I barely block his assault with my sword. I push him back enough to prepare for the next attack. I forgot how strong he is.

Zeke, I'm going to need some assistance real soon. I don't think I can take him down on my own.

One step ahead of you. Just keep him distracted. I have a plan.

I feel encouraged and channel my focus into keeping Magi's gaze on me. Zeke's going to do a sneak attack and hopefully stab this motherfucker. I block another blow aimed for my middle and twirl to the side as Magi tries to move in closer. I'm sure we look like a swirling blur to the onlooking wolves, but I don't dwell on it.

I move to take an opening on Magi's left when he fakes me out and turns. I barely manage to block him, and the force of his swing pushes me to my knees. I hold my sword steady, preparing for a hammering blow, when something warm and wet splashes across my face. I feel Magi's sword shudder against mine and I glance down from Magi's face to see a hand protruding through his chest, holding his heart.

The hand is pulled back through the gaping hole and Magi collapses. I force his weight, now leaning on my sword, off and he lands next to me. Blood pulls from his body and I cringe.

I glance up and see Zeke holding Magi's heart with a proud smile on his face. "Told you I had it covered."

I stand, frowning at the blood on my shirt. "That was gruesome." I turn and look at all the dead demons lying on the ground and then to the large group of people hovering around us. Their expressions range from surprise to fear.

"I guess we have a lot of explaining to do now," I say to Zeke as he steps to my side, still clutching Magi's heart.

"That we do." He glances around and I drop my gaze to his hand.

I scoot sideways a little from him and he whips his gaze to me. "Are you keeping that?"

"Hell yeah, I am. That's the first fallen I've ever taken out like that. This is officially a new trophy."

I glance again at his hand. "Ew."

Chapter 4

An hour later, we sit in a conference room filled with shifters from the Monroe Pack. Onyx told us the pack's name as we were escorted here. Apparently, they want to know what the heck just went down and why we're here. Yippee.

I sit, watching an older Alpha talking with a younger male, sitting on his right. I wonder if that's his son? They look similar but shouldn't he have an older son if his hair is grey?

Zeke sits next to me, Magi's heart resting in a plastic Ziplock bag. Juniper rushed to get one as soon as she spotted him with it, refusing to let him drip blood anywhere. She said we were lucky that their street was an all-shifter street. There would have been no way to hide what happened today from humans.

"Can one of you tell me why exactly there were demons on my land today? We haven't had an issue with them since I was a kid. You may call me Alpha Leon by the way." He nods at us and I'm not sure if it should be me who explains or not.

I'm saved by trying to force myself to speak by Adam standing. "Alpha Leon, it's a pleasure to meet you. My name is Adam and I'm the future Alpha of the Dark Moon pack. We sought out former pack member, Onyx Lane, regarding recent discoveries that tie back to him. We were followed by an angel and his group of demons here unbeknownst to us. We've been having issues with demons on our land in Oklahoma."

"Does this tie put my pack in danger? What information do you need from him and how will it benefit us?" Alpha Leon eyes us suspiciously.

"I hope that the information doesn't, but unfortunately, I can't trust my father. He has compromised not only my pack's safety but many others in his pursuit of power. We're here in hopes that Onyx will give us the proof we need to have the elder council remove him." Adam sighs then looks over at me. I smile, offering moral support.

Alpha Leon frowns at Adam. "Son, I think you need to give me more details than that, especially if you're going to involve the elder council. To me that screams it's a serious matter with huge repercussions. What exactly did your father do?"

"Years ago, my father sacrificed my mother to gain power with the assistance of a witch. There are only two Betas alive that may have information on what happened. I didn't find out until recently that this happened. Onyx Lane is one of the two and he's already hinted at knowing. Also, my father is moving to conquer other packs and take land. He's doing this without informing our pack and by using dark magic. We hope to warn anyone within range to prepare and possibly stop him before it progresses further."

Alpha Leon steeples his fingers together and looks at us for a few minutes with a serious expression. I hope he's thinking it over, not trying to psych us out.

"Very well. We'll assist you if you keep us informed. Onyx, do you know anything that may help these young'ins?" Alpha Leon smiles and ushers for Onyx to stand. The Alpha's sudden change in mannerisms throws me for a loop.

Onyx stands and braces his hands on the chair in front of him. He looks worried but answers his Alpha. "I do, sir. The night that Alpha Gale performed the ritual with the witch, I snuck out to follow the group. I wasn't quite in the higher ranks of Betas yet and I wanted to know what secret they were keeping. I thought it was another training session rather than what I found. The Luna, at the time, was restrained with glowing chains and held down by Beta Ralph Ward. I watched as Alpha Gale slit her throat for sacrifice and something dark burst from the ground to drink the blood. It then wrapped itself around the Alpha. It caused chaos momentarily for the group and I used that as my cover to escape. I didn't want to be caught."

Onyx pauses, as if shaking the emotions from his head. "Several days later, after a funeral for the Luna, some of the Beta's began to die via strange deaths. I knew it had something to do with that event and I placed my paperwork in to leave the pack. Not knowing I had been present, the Alpha approved, and I left. I think that's why I remain alive. To this day, none of them know I was there. These kids are the only ones who have found a tie."

The Alpha appears sad at the information Onyx shared. "Well, that does sound like a problem then. Is there a way to aid you all without letting your pack know who the informant is?"

Adam nods. "I'm sure we can find a way to keep it as secret as possible. His words confirm why Beta Ralph Ward is still alive though."

"Right. Now, why were the angels and demons following you? Do they know you're seeking information on this subject?"

I stand and their attention swings to me. "No, sir. They followed us because I brought the girl taken from our pack home. She's carrying his child. It wasn't a consensual thing."

Alpha Leon cocks his head to the side with a brow lifted. "How did he take her in the first place and why didn't your pack take care of that? You're a hellhound, right? I saw that with my own eyes."

I nod. "Yes, I'm a hellhound. Long story short, when I was kidnapped, I found a way to bring the others home. Everyone assumed she and the others were dead because of the uptick in demon attacks. Thankfully, they were all still alive, just held captive in Hell."

Alpha Leon still looks curious. "So you're from the same pack? How did that happen? I know many vampires come and go to assist packs they are friends with, so your vamp doesn't spark my interest. But you, dear, do. I've only ever met a few hellhounds in my life. That's mostly because New Orleans had demon issues when I was younger."

I sigh. "I didn't know what I was until about a year ago. I was apparently gone from this realm for a year. My mother slept with an angel before she met her mate. She didn't know what he was when it happened and then she found a way to hide me after she discovered she was pregnant."

Alpha Leon straightens. "That is fascinating, dear. I would like to stay on good terms with you. You're strong and if you're working with this future Alpha, then I do believe y'all will be great allies. My pack will do what it can to help you in your pursuit of reaching the elder council. It may take time though. I hope you understand that."

I nod as Adam speaks, "We understand, sir, and we appreciate your cooperation."

Alpha Leon nods and I sit. "Before you leave, talk to my niece, Juniper. I believe you met her briefly. She can supply you with a few things that may help you with your task of removing your father. She's half-witch and has connections. They aren't anything like what your Alpha worked with but should still be beneficial."

"Thank you, sir, we will. I appreciate you speaking with us." Adam sits.

"You're all dismissed. I do want updates on your situation soon, Adam." Alpha Leon's voice is strong, and I watch as Adam nods before we stand to leave.

Our group follows the dark mahogany floors and walls back to the front of the pack building. They have their meeting area separate from the pack house which rests on the hill behind us. This building is strictly for conferences, training, and the like, according to Onyx's words when we arrived.

We stop in the spacious front lobby at the end of the hall. It also has mahogany walls and floors. A single desk rests in the center of the room, atop a red carpet, and small sitting areas are in each corner.

Onyx grunts, getting our attention. "How about you come back to my house to talk with Juniper? I can order some pizza for us before you go."

I smile. "That would be great! I'm starving!"

"Of course, you are," Adam grumbles. "Ember, you eat more than anyone I've ever met, especially as of late."

I roll my eyes and playfully punch his arm. "Oh hush, I did use a lot of energy earlier. Magi was not an easy opponent."

"Speaking of, Zeke, what do you plan on doing with that heart?" Corey asks, looking over at Zeke.

"Well, I'm going to keep it of course. It's a trophy! I'll eventually take it to my people, and we'll preserve it. Maybe Juniper knows a preservation spell that we can use on it?" Zeke shrugs.

Seth looks serious as he says, "You better put that in a box or something then. If we get pulled over and they see that, we'll have trouble. It's too much like a human heart."

Zeke laughs. "We'll be fine. So, pizza?"

Our group laughs and Onyx leads us out the glass doors to the sidewalk before the brick building. It has vines growing up the sides, but it's been kept for the most part clean. I can see spots that have been repaired over the years, but the old building still retains its original foundation from who knows when. It's very different from the newer buildings surrounding us.

We walk down the sidewalk for about five minutes before turning down the road we fought the demons on earlier. I can see a group still cleaning up where the battle was in the distance and I'm thankful again that this street is populated by shifters. There's no way we could have kept everything hidden from prying eyes.

Juniper leans against the front porch, watching the group clean as we arrive. She nods in greeting before leading us into the house. The smell of pizza hits me as the door opens and I'm momentarily shocked that it's already here.

Seeing my look, Juniper says as I pass, "I figured you guys would be hungry, so I ordered pizza. I got a bit of everything, so help yourself to whatever you like. It's in the living room."

"Thanks, hon. We talked about doing that when we got back. You're the best." Onyx, being the last one to enter the house, pulls Juniper into his arms.

We leave them to have a moment to themselves as we make our way to the living room. Zeke moves to sit close to me as I sit on one of the couches, but I eye the bag with the heart in it, resting in his lap. I shake my head and he laughs.

"It's not like it's going to touch you, love. It's in a bag." He continues to laugh as he rests a hand on me.

I lean away slightly. "At least put it on the table or something. It's freaking me out."

The guys chuckle from across the room but I know it bothers them too.

"Fine. Are you going to fix your plate?" Zeke asks, pointing at the stack of pizza boxes.

I look at the bag with the heart and then look at the pizza boxes next to it. "Are you trying to make me lose my appetite? It's working." I push up from my chair and do my best to ignore the gruesome bag of heart and fix my plate.

I smile when I open the first box and find it covered with meat. It must be a meat lover's pizza. My stomach grumbles in happy agreement and I grab several slices before getting one of the bottles of water grouped together at the other end of the coffee table.

After I sit and dig in, Adam, Corey, and Seth all fix their plates, as Onyx and Juniper return to the room. Their cheeks are a little flushed but none of us comment on our hosts' appearance. They had a dose of unexpectedness with our arrival earlier.

"I see you guys are enjoying the pizza. Onyx mentioned that our Alpha wants me to send you with a few spells and what not to use to keep yourselves from being discovered by your Alpha. It sounds like you've got a sticky situation on your hands."

"You have no idea," I grumble between bites.

"We appreciate the help on this. I don't think it would be good for any of us to be caught. We're trying to fix things, not make them worse," Corey says, holding a large piece of cheese pizza by his mouth.

Seth and Adam nod with their mouths full and Zeke grunts. We all continue to chew our pizza while Onyx leans against the wall next to Juniper.

Juniper tosses her hair over her shoulder with a contemplative expression on her face. "Okay, I'll give you some simple things for warding and some charms for secrecy. I think I can make something for concealment. That might come in handy too. Hmm, maybe a few other things." She turns and moves back down the hall, muttering to herself as she goes. We all watch her as she goes, munching on our pizza.

Onyx looks around at us all. "So what exactly do you need me to do in regard to the elder council?"

I look at Adam, having no idea how to go about this, just that we need his witness statement. He scratches his hand and takes a minute to contemplate it before responding.

"According to the research I've done thus far, we need you to physically present it to the council. But to do that, we need to petition to see them. I'll write a letter requesting an audience with them and then contact you. This is moving much faster than I expected it to, which isn't a bad thing."

Onyx shrugs. "I guess that's not bad if we can keep your father from finding out, right? How are you going to send in a request without his notice?"

Zeke joins in, "I can help with that. The council may think it a bit odd coming from a vampire royal, but it'll get there and get their attention quicker."

Onyx looks surprised. "You're a vampire royal?"

Zeke nods. "Yes. I'm a prince. Don't share that information please. The only reason you get to know now is because it's going to get us in front of the council quicker."

Onyx holds his hands up. "No worries there, man. Wow, a royal."

Corey snorts from across the room and I look at him pointedly. We're not sharing any more than we have too.

Juniper comes bustling back into the room with a couple of bags full of items. She's smiling broadly. "Okay, so I have a ton of things for you to use and I've included some directions and a book of simple spells to use. I'm not sure if you'll be able to use them but it's worth a try. The top of the jars are color coded to the colored sheets of paper, so it'll be easier to find the directions for each. If you need anything else, you have Onyx's number. Just give us a call and we can meet up somewhere or something."

She hands me the bags and I grab them, holding them like precious cargo. "Thanks! We appreciate it."

She nods. "I'm glad I can help. I mean, I do have a bit more skin in the game than I would if you had just asked me out right. I can't let anything happen to my mate because information got leaked."

I grimace but respond, "Yeah, that's not fun. Don't worry, we won't let it happen."

"Agreed," Seth says from across the room with a growl. "Thank you both. Now, I think it's time we get out of your hair. We've got a decent drive back and a story to create about this training mission." He air quotes and we laugh.

We all stand, and Juniper and Onyx walk us to the door. Juniper hugs us and Onyx shakes our hands.

"Well, I guess we'll see you all soon. Keep us up to date on the progress so we can pass it on to our Alpha. Drive safe!" Onyx says as we step from his porch.

"Thanks, we will!" Seth calls over his shoulder.

We make it to the SUV, and I point out the black ooze on the window. "We need to hit up a car wash before we get back. We don't want to carry that back into pack territory."

"Right." Seth looks at the spot and frowns.

We climb in and get situated. After we've driven for about ten minutes, Zeke says, "Shit, I forgot to ask her about a preservation spell."

I look at him and notice the gruesome bag in his lap. "You also forgot to ask for a box. Ew. Let me dig around in those bags and see if there is something that we can use."

I turn around and reach for the bags I tucked into the very back after climbing in. I dig around and find the book and a small binder with colored pages. I turn around and begin thumbing through the book and find a spell for short preservation and one for cloaking.

"Holy shit, she really did give us a good variety. I have one to preserve it and cloak it until we make it back. That's if I can get the spell to work." I shrug and look at the bag with the heart.

"Well, love, if any of us can pull one off, I think you have a higher chance, having angel magic and all. Try it out." Zeke encourages me with a smile, and I look at the book.

Scanning over the preservation spell, I see that I need to hold the item and repeat the words three times. I grab the nasty heart and set it in my lap, grimacing as I read from the book aloud.

"I call to thee,
Oh, blessed be,
To preserve this item,
Temporarily,
May you hear my call,
So, mote it be."

I say the words three times as the book directs and feel a cooling sensation move down my spine. It sends chills down my arms, and I feel my hands warm. I stare at the gruesome heart as it glows faintly with a yellow light.

"Holy shit, you did it!" Corey says from the seat in front of me where he's staring at the heart.

Adam and Seth glance back from the front with curious expressions. I shrug and flip the pages of the book back to the cloaking spell. The description makes me think of what I do with my wings. I look over the words, still holding the heart in its bag before reading them aloud in the same manner. It directs me to envision what I want it to appear after repeating the words three times.

"Hide it well
Even the smell
Don't let them see
Unless they truly believe
What I have
Is just unseen."

I close my eyes and picture a tan purse like what my mother carries. It's got golden clasps and a long strap. Opening my eyes, I feel the magic surge from my hands and gape as the heart flickers and turns into a purse.

"Well, I think we're good now. When are you taking this to Hell? I don't think you should keep it around long." I hand the purse to Zeke who eyes it curiously.

"I'm not sure honestly. It depends on how things go in the next week. I'll put it in the freezer and just ask your mom not to touch it." Zeke shrugs and relaxes back into his seat.

"I don't see that going well. If it looks like one of our purses, she'll try to move it, thinking someone's being pranked. I think you should tell her but I guess we'll figure that out when we get back." My stomach growls and I hear a grumble toward the front of the car.

"Was that your stomach again, Ember? We just ate!" Adam turns in his seat to glare at me.

"Hey, I just did magic. I guess it works like my other magic does. I don't know. I can wait until our halfway stop. Don't worry." I smile at him, and Seth laughs while keeping his eyes on the road.

"You all are hilarious. Hang tight and relax. We'll be back soon enough," he says, chuckling.

We all sit back, and I ignore the grumbles of my stomach as I watch the trees and houses fly by out the window. We accomplished more on this trip than I expected.

Chapter 5

Zeke and I sit in the living room, and I listen to him try to explain to my mom what he's put in our freezer. She's pissed and the two have been bickering about it back and forth. My sisters are asleep upstairs, having worked extra hard today at training and then going for a run before dinner. I'm proud of how well they're doing.

Dad sits across from me on the couch next to Mom with an amused expression on his face. He knows better than to interfere when Zeke gets to arguing with her. They have been friends for years.

I stretch and relax into the couch. Today has been a long day. It's hard to believe we went all the way to Louisiana and back. Alpha Gale accepted our story of discovering a wayward pack of green demons and taking them out. He was excited that we took the courage to branch out on our own to improve our teamwork skills and train, but I didn't miss Adam's cringe as his dad patted him on the back and pulled him into a hug. It hurt my heart, but we must maintain a normal appearance. I don't know how their relationship will be once the elder council gets involved.

As I'm snuggling up to Zeke, now that he and my mom have stopped arguing, a knock on the front door causes us to stiffen.

"Are we expecting anyone?" my mother asks, looking at Zeke and me. We shake our heads.

I listen, trying to pick up on who may be there but all I can hear are two steady heartbeats. Maybe it's Adam and Corey, although I should at least be able to hear them conversing or scent them.

My dad stands. "I'll go answer the door. Hang tight."

We watch him move down the hall toward the front door until he's out of sight. I hear him open the door and a deep voice asks, "Does Kyra live here?" A loud growl follows.

I look at my mom who's gone pale. I then look at Zeke who's extremely stiff. I turn back toward the hall and listen again.

"Yes, she does. This isn't a great time though. Can I have her call you? What is your name?" My dad sounds aggravated, and I fear what might happen next.

"Well, really, I'm here to see my daughter, Ember, but I thought it would be rude to ask for her straight out since I didn't know she existed until recently. Now, may I come in or are you really going to make the king of Hell linger on your doorstep?"

My eyes widen and I whip my head around to look at my mom. Zeke grabs my hand and I listen as my dad leads Lucifer down the hall. There is another pair of footsteps with him.

We all stare as my dad enters the living room, anger written across his face. My heart stutters at the amber-eyed male behind Lucifer. His dark hair is tied back behind his ears and his strong jaw is set. I recognize him instantly and I feel the pull between us grow stronger as Kai meets my gaze.

Lucifer takes a seat on the third empty couch. He wears a black suit, and his hair is styled. His wings are hidden but the scar over his right eye stands out. I force myself to quit looking at Kai as he stands to the side of the couch with his arms across his chest and meet Lucifer's gaze.

Lucifer looks at my mother. "Kyra, you're as beautiful as ever. I'm shocked you've kept my daughter a secret like this for so long, but then again, I'm thankful. Unlike my other offspring, she's grown up to be a fighter. It's time for her to come with me."

My mother turns bright red. I'm not sure if it's from anger or if she's blushing until she speaks. "Like hell you'll take her. Her life is here!"

"Mom," I say, getting her attention. Everyone looks at me. "I knew this was coming, remember? It's okay. You guys will be fine."

Lucifer quirks up a brow. "What is it they have to be worried about?"

I turn my gaze to Kai. "Did you not tell him?"

He looks stunned that I would address him. "I told him that he had a daughter. What else was I supposed to tell him?"

I look to Lucifer. "Well, Lucifer, what Kai left out was that Greed is stirring up a lot of trouble for my pack and so are his little soldier groupies. There are also demons that keep attacking for some reason and all we can do is assume it's tied to Greed."

Lucifer places a hand under his chin. "Interesting. I did hear about a tussle at his castle during the ball. Does that have anything to do with it?"

"Ugh, yeah! I was escaping my imprisonment! Did Kai not tell you that either? There were a ton of female shifters I helped rescue as well. Does that kind of thing just go unnoticed? What kind of place are you running?" I ask incredulously, looking between Kai and Lucifer.

"I had no idea that was happening. I do apologize, daughter. I suspected something was up when Greed invited me to his castle. It's been ages since he's done that." Lucifer looks at me curiously.

"Well, maybe you should pay more attention to what's going on. He's been doing a lot and is planning to overthrow you." I cross my arms and sit back. Zeke moves his hand to rest it on my leg. It's reassuring.

Lucifer's face flushes. "How do you know this information?"

I glare at Kai and then look to Lucifer. "I was a prisoner there and forced to pretend I had no memories after one of my mates helped me unlock them. Prospero shared a lot of details about his father's plans and his hellhound army."

Kai's face turns red at those words, and I smile smugly as Lucifer turns to look at him. "Did you know any of this?"

Kai looks to Lucifer. "No, sir. None of that was mentioned when I helped them escape at the gate."

"Well then, this is more reason for you to join me, dear. Your mate may join of course if I approve." He looks at Zeke. "I take it Prince Ezekiel is your mate?"

I nod and rein in my emotions. "He's one of them. I have three."

Lucifer's eyes light up. "Three? Impressive. I've never even had one that I've known of. Who are they? I must approve of them all."

I feel Zeke squeeze my hand in encouragement and swallow. "Why do you need to approve of my mates to have them at your castle?"

Lucifer watches me curiously. "Because I must be able to trust them. Now, who are they?"

"Well, you're correct, Zeke is one. Another is Prince Ulric, Greed's son. The third, well, I'm not sure if he knows yet or not. I found out on a brief encounter where I almost died, and he was there." I shrug and meet

Kai's gaze. His eyes are wide, and it seems that he understands.

Lucifer follows my gaze and looks at Kai's wide-eyed one. He bursts out laughing as realization sinks in. "Oh, this is just wonderful. Kai, you've finally found a mate after all these centuries and it's of my own flesh and blood." He turns to look at me cheerily. "I approve, daughter. Now go pack your things. We need to leave."

I gape, looking at him and then to Kai who remains stunned. Zeke squeezes my hand, so I turn to look at him. He smiles. Feeling confused, I turn back to Lucifer. "What exactly do I need to pack?"

My parents have remained silent this entire time and finally Mom chimes in. "Just pack as if you're going on a regular trip. It'll be nice having some of your things there unlike before, I'm sure."

I look at her and notice tears in her eyes. I stand and move to her and let her embrace me. She holds me and I feel my dad slide his arms around us both.

"It'll be okay. I promise, I'll be fine. I'll come back soon," I say, hugging them tighter.

"We know, honey. It's just not easy on us. We thought you would be close forever. Remember, time works differently here than it does in Hell," my mother says and she and my dad pull back.

"I remember." I stand and look at Lucifer. "Okay, I'll start packing. I guess just make yourself comfortable."

Lucifer sits back and motions for Kai to sit as well. He looks uncomfortable and eyes my parents warily. It's like he doesn't know what to do with the news that he has a mate.

I grab Zeke's hand and he walks with me down the hall toward my room. Before reaching my door, I stop and push my sisters' door open. They open their eyes as the light spills in and sit up, looking at me confused.

"Hey, sorry to wake you. Can I come in?" I ask and I feel Zeke move past me. He must be going to my room.

"Yeah, what's up?" Winnie asks, moving so I can sit on her bed.

Tansy moves from her bed to sit with us.

"Well, you remember how I said I would eventually have to return to Hell? It's time. Lucifer is downstairs and I'm to pack.

"Wow," Tansy says and moves to turn on the lamp light. "Well, I guess we're getting up. There's no way we're missing meeting the king of Hell or telling you goodbye. Do you need help packing?"

Winnie blinks at us, trying to comprehend things. I'm shocked Tansy is taking it so well.

"I can handle it. If you guys want to go downstairs, you can. I'll be down soon." I hug them both and stand up. They smile at me as I move toward the door.

"Okay, we'll be down when you're ready. We love you, Ember," Winnie says tearfully and I move in to hug her again.

"I love you both, too. I'll be down in a few. I better text Corey and Adam. Probably Seth too. They're going to make sure you guys stay safe while I'm gone."

"Please," Winnie says. "We can handle ourselves."

Tansy chuckles and tosses a robe at Winnie. "We still have a lot to learn. Go pack, Ember."

I smile and move out of the door and down the hall. Zeke is moving around the room, grabbing things and putting them in a bag. "I texted the guys already. All three are on their way as we speak. Listen, when we get to Lucifer's, I'm going to make a trip to my kingdom. I want to see if I can find anything out about Zuko and Ulric. Maybe they both survived."

I move toward my dresser and start grabbing things. "That sounds like a good idea. Maybe I'll be able to feel him when we're back. I'm more worried about things here. Do you think Adam and Corey can handle the elder council thing by themselves?"

Zeke pauses. "Shit, I forgot about that. I've got to take his request to the council. Okay, new plan. I can't go with you tonight if we want that request to get there in time. Are you okay with that?"

I pause and meet Zeke's gaze. "I think I can be. I promised we would help however we could. You know how to find me in Hell, right?" I gulp and Zeke senses my concern.

He moves to me and wraps me in his arms. "Yes. I'll come to you as soon as I can. You know I will. Maybe it'll give Kai time to warm up to you. He didn't seem to take the news well."

I roll my eyes. "Yeah. If he doesn't accept me, we'll figure it out. I'm sure it won't kill me if he denies me, right?"

"It shouldn't. Now let's get you packed."

§

A short time later, with two large duffels full of things to take with me, Zeke helps me drag my bags down the hall. I heard the door earlier but tried not to listen intently as the guys came in and met Lucifer.

As I enter the room, I can feel the tension. It's so thick that it makes me feel like swimming through peanut butter. Corey, Adam, and Seth glower at Lucifer and Kai from across the room as Kai and Lucifer lean against the wall closest to my family resting on the couch. My sisters eye Lucifer and Kai warily. Kai glares at the guys from where he remains close to Lucifer, who looks amused. They turn to me as I plop the large duffel I'm carrying on the ground, and Zeke pauses next to me.

"Did I miss something?" I ask, looking between the two groups.

Corey snorts before he says, "No, it's just awkward because we're pissed that you're leaving and these two aren't being the most pleasant to have a conversation with. Your new mate isn't much of a talker."

I look at Kai who continues to glare at the guys. Sensing me looking at him, he flicks his gaze to me. He doesn't say a word but lets his glare drop some. He's obviously ticked about something.

I shrug. "So is everything squared away for my absence. Did you guys get a plan figured out for all the things?" I air quote as I say things and look mainly at Adam.

He nods. "We did. Is there a way we can communicate with you while you're in Hell so we can keep you up to date on things?"

I look at Lucifer and he lifts a brow. "Why do you need to keep in contact with her about pack matters? She's going to be training to rule Hell. That's more important."

I cringe because I didn't want that topic coming up. I've been skittering over it briefly and trying to avoid it at all costs.

I feel the tension thicken as my mom speaks up. "She's going to do what?"

"Okay, so I figured this may happen, but I'm also tied to this pack. You will find a way to set up communication or I won't be going. Deal?" I cross my arms and glare at Lucifer.

"Who said you had a choice in the matter?" Lucifer declares and growls fill the room. Kai tenses for a fight beside Lucifer and I know this could easily go sideways.

"Easy, guys. No need to alert anyone that things are going down. It's going to be weird enough explaining to Alpha Gale that Lucifer showed up in the middle of the night to get me." I growl after I speak.

"Fine, I'll set something up. Once we get there, I'll establish something akin to your mail system. Will that work?" Lucifer asks with a stern expression.

"Is there not anything faster? I mean, it's the twenty-first century here and we have cell phones. We can easily call someone up as needed," Corey says, and Lucifer looks at him like he's grown two heads.

"Was there anything in that book Juniper gave you about a communication spell by chance?" Seth asks, bringing Lucifer's attention away from Corey.

"I'll go grab it. You left it in the kitchen, right?" Zeke asks and I nod. He zooms out and quickly returns with the book.

I flip it open and scan through its contents. Toward the back of the book, I find something about communication through mirrors. It needs the hair of the person or persons you want to communicate with, mirrors, salt, a white candle, dried basil, and a small bowl of water. I have to light the candle between the two mirrors and sprinkle all the items minus the basil on them. Then I light the basil and move the smoke over the mirrors as I chant the words.

"This looks promising. How many compact mirrors do we have around the house?" I ask, looking at my mom and sisters.

They blink back at me before getting up to retrieve what they have. I send the guys through the house with my dad to get the other ingredients. Lucifer watches on curiously.

"Okay, set everything down in the middle of the room. I need hair from everyone who wishes to set up a line of communication on each mirror. Then I'll start the spell," I say, pointing to the pile of mirrors lying on the floor.

"Have you done this before?" Lucifer asks, standing from his chair. "You shouldn't need to use a spell for this if your magic is strong enough. Then again, you must know how to use it for what you want."

"Thanks for the encouragement but no. I did my first spell today. I didn't know what I could use my power for. I only got some brief lessons before. Do you want me to continue with what I'm doing, or will you set the mirrors up?" I'm agitated that he's just now sharing this information.

He waves his hand at the items. "Continue. I want to see what happens."

I roll my eyes and watch as everyone adds their hair, including Lucifer and Kai. Weird. I try not to question it though as I add mine to the piles and step back. I light the candle and start burning the basil, moving the smoke over the mirrors with my hand. I look at the book and repeat the words from its pages three times.

"Mirror, Mirror,
Let me see
Those connected to me
Through this lens

Show me their eyes
So, we may communicate
Safely as if nigh
So Mote It Be."

I close my eyes and feel my magic trickle out of me toward the mirrors. It's a strange sensation and feels like water dripping down my spine. Once the sensation stops, I open my eyes and look at the mirrors. All the items are gone, and the mirrors glow faintly with a white light. I'm glad they have tops. It'll be easier to hide them.

"Well, I think we're good. Everyone take one." I wave at the mirrors, sighing. I feel tired suddenly.

"That was quite impressive. I guess I need to add a time for you to work with one of my witches to your agenda." Lucifer glides closer and rests his hand on my shoulder. "Now, we need to go. It's quite a drive from here to New Orleans. That's where the closest gate is."

I cringe, first at the idea of a planned agenda and then at the thought of driving that far. I keep my mouth shut though and begin to make my way through the room, sharing goodbyes. I'm emotional but I force myself to hold it in. I need to be strong for my family. It's going to be difficult for them for a while.

"Promise me you will keep them all safe, Adam." I pause and pull out of our hug.

He looks me in the eye and kisses me on the cheek. "I promise, Ember. Stay safe and let us know when you arrive. These damn mirrors better work."

I nod and hug him again. Zeke is the last one I say goodbye to. "I will be there as soon as I can. I promise. I'll make sure things are going smoothly here first."

"I know. Be safe. I love you, Zeke." I reach up on my toes and kiss him.

He returns the kiss and I ache at the idea of being separated. This is going to be rough.

I pull back and he grabs both of my bags. I turn and see Kai facing toward the door as Lucifer looks at me in amusement.

"I'll lead you to the car. Prince Ezekiel, I'll be expecting you soon. She's in good hands." Lucifer smiles smugly at Zeke and I roll my eyes. I feel like he's torturing Kai but at the same time, Kai seems frustrated that he has a mate. Why?

"I believe you, sir." Zeke nods and we stop before a small black

Infiniti Q50.

The black exterior reflects the stars beautifully. Kai unlocks the car and Lucifer slides into the front passenger seat. The interior is black as well. I hear the trunk pop and I move to it with Zeke, to place my bags within.

I give him a lingering kiss, fighting tears after he closes the trunk. "You're going to be okay, love. I'll see you soon."

"It's a lot to process." I wipe at my eyes. "I'm going to miss everyone but at least we have the mirrors to talk unlike last time. This is difficult though."

"We can do this, love. Now, let's not detain the king of Hell any longer. I love you."

"I love you too. Thank you, Zeke." I hug him one last time before I move around and climb into the backseat.

I close the door and glance at the front where Kai sits watching me with a stony expression. I lift my brow and he looks away. Lucifer looks smug as he relaxes back and pulls a book out of the center console. I'm not sure how he can see but maybe that's a trait we have? I haven't tried it yet.

I turn and glance out of the window as we pull away. The lights of the house seem bright, and I let my tears fall silently. My heart pulses and I feel Zeke's soft caress through our connection as he sends me reassuring vibes. It helps, but the tears continue to fall.

Chapter 6

I wake, who knows how long later, to the car stopping. I didn't even realize I'd fallen asleep. I guess my emotions wore me out. I sit up straight, having dozed off against the window and notice Kai unbuckling himself in the seat in front of me. Lucifer is doing the same and I realize we're parked in front of an old Victorian-style home.

It's still dark outside but I can tell that the lawn is taken care of regularly and that there are fresh flowers growing in the flower beds along the huge steps leading to the front door. Concrete gargoyles rest at the end of the steps and I watch them suspiciously for a moment. Are they real or fake?

Kai opens his door and I whip around and ask aloud, "Where are we?"

Lucifer responds as Kai closes the door. "New Orleans. You slept hard back there. We're dropping off the car and walking the rest of the way on foot. I've already informed Kai he'll be carrying your bags. He's taking the mate thing hard. It's a long story for a later date though. We need to get moving."

I blink a few times, trying to process his words and nod in response before climbing out of the back of the car. My brain is still in a sleep fog. I turn to look at the back of the vehicle and notice Kai has both duffels slung over his shoulders. He watches me warily but doesn't say a word.

I mentally poke at the bond that formed between the two of us only to find a wall. I guess he's had plenty of time to practice blocking. Fine.

I roll my eyes and move around to the side of the car where Lucifer stands, looking up at the house. I follow his gaze and spot a woman with blond hair peeking through the curtains. She waves and then closes them quickly. Lucifer smiles as she disappears and begins walking down the sidewalk.

I follow in silence, sensing Kai trailing behind me. This is all so strange but then again, I didn't know what to expect when they came for me. I guess it's better than being forced to do things or taking my memories.

We walk along the dimly lit sidewalk for a solid ten minutes before Lucifer leads us toward a small park area. The trees are trimmed, and bushes line the sidewalk on both sides. A large fountain rests in the middle of it and we make our way toward it.

I stop at the fountain and watch as Lucifer steps in. He doesn't pause but holds up his hand. A gate shimmers to life.

"Are you kidding me? The gate is in a fountain?" I ask aloud, and Lucifer looks over his shoulder at me.

"At one point in time, it wasn't in this fountain, but since humans can't see them, things like this happen. Now, let's go." He turns and steps through the gate with a loud pop and I let out a sigh.

"Is there a way to not get my feet wet as I walk to the gate?" I ask Kai over my shoulder, and he frowns.

"Suck it up, buttercup. You'll be fine," he says and ushers me forward.

"Wow, I'm impressed you know that saying. Do you come to this realm often?" I lift both brows as I tentatively step into the water. It's warm thankfully, but it soaks my jeans and shoes. I hope they dry easily.

"I do quite a bit in this realm. You'll learn in time. Now, can you please move?" he growls and I roll my eyes.

"So pushy." I turn and face the gate in front of me as I continue to trudge through the water. This gate sucks.

I push through the swirling colors of the gate and momentarily lose my breath as I feel like I'm falling. It's disorienting. Finally when I feel solid ground beneath my feet, I collapse. I look around and notice mountains surrounding me. Lucifer stands on a stone path ahead of me. He looks bored.

"Took you long enough," he says as Kai appears beside me. He grunts and I push up from the dirt.

Dusting myself off, I ask, "Where are we?"

Lucifer smiles. "Oh, we're almost to my estate. It's just around the bend here. The portals can be manipulated to pop you out where you please if you know how to work them. The location must be to another portal though. This is the one closest to home."

He sets off walking, turning his back to me, and Kai moves forward behind him, still carrying my bags. I shrug, not having a chance to respond to Lucifer's words and follow along.

The landscape is a vibrant green and the dark sky overhead doesn't freak me out like it did on my first trip to Hell. It's beautiful and lighter, signifying sunrise for this realm. Trees, like pines, jot up from the greenery around me. It makes me laugh how Hell is often portrayed as a burning landscape when really, it's another version of earth. Except for the few lava rivers, one which catches my eye as the castle comes into view.

"Holy shit, is that seriously lava?" I ask stunned and Kai grunts.

"That is, yes. The River Styx lies further out from it on the other side," Lucifer says over his shoulder and continues to walk.

The lava river winds along the far-right side of the estate. The estate itself reminds me of a fancy mansion. It's large with white brick and black trim. It's properly cared for with flowers blooming everywhere. It's quite impressive and modern.

As we near, Lucifer passes through a forested arch to a garden and leads us straight through to the back of the estate. I admire the various flowers and other blooming plants as we pass. They remind me of Persephone's garden at Greed's castle. Maybe she visits often?

Suddenly, I realize I can check and see if I'm still connected to Ulric. Is he alive? I mentally reach down to where my heart is to the connections I have with my mates. The one tying me to Kai is strong but not finished. It's dim like it needs to be charged. I feel for the one between Zeke and I and notice it's strong but not as if we were on the same plane. My heart plummets as I realize I can still feel him in this plane of existence, but I'm not able to feel Ulric.

Fighting the fear that tries to bubble up, I keep searching and finally a faint pulsing, almost as if the link to Ulric has been damaged. Does that mean he's dead? My stomach knots and my pulse quickens.

I try to send a thought down it, but nothing happens. It just flickers and seems to fall asleep. What the hell? This causes my stomach to plummet.

I focus on Lucifer as he leads us to a small wooden door and try to push my emotions back. I can't let myself lose focus right now. I'll try to mess with my connections later once I know where my room is. I should have privacy then.

He pushes through the door, and I follow but the exterior makes me stop in my tracks. Everything is modernized and tasteful. There is plush carpet and electricity. Is that air conditioning?

I stand transfixed at the industrial-style interior. "You have electricity?" I stammer out.

Lucifer laughs. "Of course, we have electricity. Why wouldn't we? Magic runs some things but there's no sense in passing up modern-day conveniences."

"It's just, Greed didn't." I start walking again.

"That's by his own choice. Although he probably enjoys having magic run more of his castle than any of the others. We'll show you to your room and let you rest. This afternoon, your training begins. Kai will escort you." Lucifer smiles smugly at Kai. "I have business to attend to."

Kai groans and says, "This way."

I look between the two, at the lack of formality, since he was all yes sir, no sir earlier. Whatever.

He leads me down a hall that veers to the left. Gorgeous paintings hang from the walls on either side and an occasional bench rests against the wall. We pass a stone pillar with a blue vase resting atop it and turn right to ascend a small set of stairs. They spiral up and take us to another floor like the last.

We move down it and I notice it's more spacious. There are large doors spaced evenly apart.

Kai stops before a double set and pushes it open. I gape at the cream-colored carpet and matching set of couches. "This is your room. Someone will come fetch you this afternoon."

He walks through the doors, and I take in how beautiful everything is. There are light purple accents throughout the room with fresh flowers. A crystal chandelier hangs above a small table and chairs with a kitchenette.

Kai leads me into another room with a large canopy bed. It's massive and has the same color scheme. He plops my bags on the bed and turns to leave with a brief nod. No goodbye or see you later, he just leaves.

Okay then. I turn to the bed and stare at my bags. I do feel tired.

My emotions raise their heads and I kick off my shoes. Pulling back the covers, I let the tears fall once again. My emotions tingle down my bonds, but I block the connection after taking a minute to focus. I let the tears fall until I doze off.

§

The sound of someone knocking on the door wakes me hours later and I wake slightly disoriented. I look around, taking in the canopy bed again and the carpet, and realize I'm in Hell. Right. "Come in," I say and push off the mattress.

I make my way across the carpet and enter the sitting area. I'm startled when an angel with silver wings and black hair streaked with the same color enters. She has an air of authority about her and she's also gorgeously curvy.

She smiles at me as she closes the door and makes a small bow. "Hello, Ember, my name is Arminda, and I'm to be of assistance to you. I will be your tutor or governess of sorts. I'm here to discuss your agenda with you before taking you to explore your new residence."

I blink, taking in everything she just said, and I point to the small table and chairs. "Shall we sit and talk there? I'd offer you something to drink but I'm not sure what is here yet. I fell asleep after arriving."

"No worries, I'll assist you with that. Your room should be fully stocked. We prepared early for your arrival. I believe there is an electric tea kettle and tea bags in that cabinet." Arminda points to the cabinet on the far right above the small sink.

I make my way over as I respond, "Excellent. I'll whip us up some."

She moves to the table and grabs a chair. "I do believe there is a coffee pot there too if you prefer that. I'm more of a tea drinker but for future reference and all."

"Oh, thank Goddess. I'll make you some tea and I'll have a cup of coffee. Nothing against tea but the coffee flavor suits me better." I smile as I open the cabinet and find exactly what she said I would. There is a variety of tea flavors and coffee flavors stacked next to the electric tea kettle and small coffee pot.

As if sensing my next question she says, "Just fix me some of the peach, please."

"Did you just read my mind?" I ask, looking over my shoulder and she laughs.

"No, I had a guess that you would ask. I helped stock everything. There are fruits and vegetables as well as other small items in your refrigerator. Most of your meals will be served in Lucifer's private dining hall. I'll show you where that is later."

She quiets and I busy myself making our drinks. I find cups for the hot beverages in another cabinet and grab a plate to stick some of the fruit she mentioned on. Snacks are always good.

"Here we go," I say as I place everything on the small table and take a seat across from her. "So, what's first?"

She sips at her tea and then sets her cup down to cool. "Today, you will have a tour of the estate and dine later with your father. I will help you unpack and give you some reading material. It's time for you to start learning some history about Hell. Not the stuff they teach on earth. I assume you know manners, having come from a pack that's been prepping you to be Luna all your life. We will still review some techniques." She pauses to take a sip of her tea.

"Should I get a notebook to take notes?" I ask, worry sinking its teeth into me.

"No, we'll go over what is needed tomorrow. Your day will start with me going through a review. Then you'll attend training with the hellhounds down at the barracks. Once completed there, you'll attend classes with various teachers. For this first week, you'll be meeting with Minerva for early lessons on witchcraft. Lucifer added that first thing when he got back today. You'll also have lessons with me in history as well as other matters. You'll begin reading the required books tonight."

I stare at her, trying to prepare my brain to be a sponge. This is going to be worse than what college would have been like.

She snaps her fingers, drawing me from my thoughts, and a stack of books appears on the table between us. They are old and leather bound with stained pages. Their smell is also different from what you find with old books. These smell of salt, earth, and blood.

"What are those books made of?" I ask curiously, as she picks the one on top of the pile up gently.

She runs a hand across the cover. "Some are made from demon skins and similar bodies. They have been spelled to hold for eternity. You don't have to worry about decay while you have them."

"Is that normal?" I ask stunned.

"Not anymore, no. Lucifer changed the laws to forbid that decades ago. Now, we simply use parchment or paper like humans. It's easier to copy." She slides the book across the table and rests it in front of me.

"Is this one of the demon-skinned ones?" I pick up the book and smell it. It stinks.

"It is, but it's one of the best on the beginnings of Hell. It's still being transferred to paper. I want you to begin reading this tonight and in three days' time, I want a write-up on the first ten chapters. You will tell me the highlights and then I will give you a fun quiz. I'll lecture over the first two chapters tomorrow." She snaps her fingers again and a small laptop appears with a printer. It lands and then a handful of other office supplies appear next to it.

"Holy shit. This is going to be like school all over again," I say astounded.

"Of course it is. You have a lot to learn. Now, before you get too comfortable, finish your coffee. We need to get moving on the tour. We must not be late for dinner." She looks at me sternly.

I pick up my cup and down the hot contents, enjoying the feel of it hitting my throat. Setting the cup down, I say, "Right, let's do this."

I quickly stand from my chair, not missing the eye roll Arminda throws in my direction. This should be fun, right?

She stands gracefully. "I want you to work on being fluid and graceful from now on when you move. You're not an awkward teenager but an immortal. A very high born one at that."

I stare at her as my mind drifts to the movie *Miss Congeniality*. Is she going to try to change how I do everything?

"Let's go. We'll start with the area around the throne room and end in the gardens. Once done, I'll swing you back around to Lucifer's dining room which is located down the hall."

"Oh, that's close. Is his room in this hall too?"

"Indeed, his rooms are two doors down. This floor is for the family, or those Lucifer considers as such."

I nod in understanding, and she proceeds to lead from the hall.

Chapter 7

Hours later, I all but collapse into a chair seated at Lucifer's table. He looks at me curiously as I rub my head and reach for the glass of wine in front of me. I'm thankful it's there even if I've never been a huge fan.

"Rough day?" he asks as I'm about to take a sip from the glass.

I finish taking a sip and notice the wine is better than I expected. A little bitter but the flavor is good with a strange hint of chocolate and spices. "Covering the castle and trying to remember where things are was hard, so yes. Also, there are a lot of things I'm expected to do. Walk a certain way and such."

"Oh yes. I forget that Arminda is a stickler about that. You'll get the hang of it. What did you think of the estate?"

"It's beautiful. I especially love the garden. Arminda mentioned Persephone helped create it. Does she live close?"

"Somewhat, yes. She and Hades live on the other side of the mountains. They visit often. I'll introduce you soon. I may plan a dinner to officially present you or possibly a ball."

I frown, recalling the events of the most recent ball I attended. That didn't turn out very well. "Will you invite all of the fallen?"

He seems to contemplate that for a second. "I'm not sure yet. Maybe. We'll see."

I nod and look up as several men and women enter, carrying plates and dishes. They set the food before us on the table, and I sigh in relief as I notice a normal-looking steak and several side dishes such as potatoes, green beans, and salad.

"Did Arminda mention a schedule to you earlier?" Lucifer asks as he cuts his steak.

I shrug, picking at my food. "She did. It's a little intense but I guess I'm okay with it."

"It'll settle down in time. If Greed is preparing something, I want you to be in top form to help me lead our troops. You'll need to use all your abilities to do that. I may set you up with extra training for your hellhound abilities. You could strengthen our ranks that way." He smiles smugly and takes a sip of his wine.

"Wouldn't Kai be upset? He doesn't seem too keen about me being his mate. What's his deal?"

"He'll be fine. He finally settled with never having a mate, so it startled him. Things will be easier after you get to know each other."

"Do you think so?"

"Yes. How is the food?"

I look at my near-empty plate. "It's delicious."

"Good, finish up so you can call your friends. They've been trying to contact you through the mirrors. The one I've kept on me has been heating up on occasion."

"Shit, I forgot to call them when we arrived. Thanks for the reminder." I quickly finish my plate and stand. "See you tomorrow, Lucifer."

He lifts a brow at me. "Goodnight, Ember."

I take my leave and enter the hall. Thankfully, my room is close, so I sprint the short distance from the dining hall door to my room. I make my way across the sitting area to my room with my bags. I dig around in the one I tucked the mirror into and pull it out.

I place it in my palm and open it. It's warm as I close my eyes and envision my friends' faces.

"Hey, Em, it's about time you contacted us. We were starting to worry." I open my eyes and see Zeke, Corey, and Adam's faces in the small compact.

"I'm so sorry. I fell asleep after we arrived, and my tutor showed up to give me a tour. How are things?" I ask and reach within myself to tug at my connection to Zeke. It feels stronger.

Zeke smiles at me from the mirror. "Well, Alpha Gale is pissed that you're gone. We didn't give him much detail other than that you're in Hell again."

"I think he was planning something, so it's good. Zeke is taking our letter to the elder council in a few days," Adam says.

"Good, I'm glad things are on track still. Will you contact Onyx before or after you take it?" I look more at Zeke's image.

"After. So, how is your connection to Ulric? Is it there? I felt you tug at ours." Zeke says.

I frown, checking again, and notice there's still no change. "Honestly, I feel something there but it's different. I still can't tell if he's dead or alive."

Zeke's expression becomes contemplative. "Maybe he was injured more than we thought? I'll leave for my kingdom as soon as we get this council business finished."

I nod. "How's my family?"

Corey clears his throat. "They're good. You should try to call them later and chat. Your sisters miss you. It's been a few days here."

I shake my head. "Time is so weird between realms. I'll call them tomorrow. I have a busy schedule starting in the morning. I've got to get some rest before then and start my reading."

Adam smirks. "I doubt it's anything you can't handle. I mean, you've been prepping to be Luna for years. It can't be much different, right?"

I roll my eyes. "From what Arminda, my tutor told me, it's challenging. I have extra things to study. We'll see how it goes tomorrow."

"You'll do great, love." Zeke winks at me.

"Thanks. Okay, I'll call again soon. I'll keep my mirror on me from now on. Bye, guys!" I smile into the mirror.

I get a resounding goodbye from them and hear Zeke whisper down our connection, *I love you.*

I love you too, Zeke, I send in response and close the mirror.

I stand and set the mirror on the small nightstand next to my bed and dig in my duffel for something to wear to sleep. I place the shorts and t-shirt on the bed after pulling them out from the bottom of the bag.

Twirling my hair, I make my way to the bathroom and pause to gape at all the granite. It's a gorgeous cream tone to match the rest of the small living quarters. Fancy white towels hang on golden rods across the room and a large tub is sunk into the floor. Several showerheads hang above it. I shed my clothes and set my feet on the floor, noticing how warm it feels, and giggle. Is it possible there are those fancy floor warmers installed like

I've seen on HGTV? Wow!

I turn the water on and let it heat, noticing the variety of soaps for me to use. I already feel spoiled just staring at them. Stepping into the water, I let it fall over me, imagining it washing away all my negativity, and cleansing my soul. It feels magical. I close my eyes and lean against the wall. I feel as if I'm ready to tackle the next couple of days now.

Chapter 8

I wake to the sound of someone moving around my room and I lurch out of bed, looking for an attacker. I blink, trying to clear the sleep from my eyes while listening intently. A light chuckle catches my attention and I turn to find Arminda hanging clothes in my closet. My bags rest at her feet.

"Now that you're up, you can dress in one of the new outfits I had made for you. I had a pair of silk pants made and fitted tops that will allow you to display your wings. You don't have to hide them here since they're proof of your heritage. I also retrieved several pairs of leather boots that are flexible and easy to move in from the tailor. The dresses I have placed in here are for when you're not training. They have matching shoes."

I focus and let my cloaking down. It's become a habit to keep it up. She's right about not needing to hide them. "Ever since they showed up, I've pretty much had to hide them. So, the new silk clothes, will they hold up in training?"

"They will. Even though they're silk, they've been spelled to hold unless cut with a spelled weapon. It works as a fail safe for training because if that happens, we know someone is truly trying to hurt you." She smiles as she hangs up another outfit.

"What if we're training with spelled weapons?" I ask and pull one of the aforementioned outfits out and begin to dress.

"Hm, I guess I can have others made. I'll talk to the seamstress. We have other materials that will look luxurious on you. Now, let's do a quick review of the layout of the estate while you dress."

"Just the estate?" I ask, pulling the top over my head and wings.

"Yes, I can tell you didn't pick up the book I asked you to read but I'm sure you'll work on it today. After all, we'll be going over the first chapter this afternoon once you've finished with training and your witchery class."

I groan and move toward the bathroom to tie my hair back. Arminda follows. She asks me to tell her where we visited yesterday, and which floor of the estate certain rooms are on. She asks me several other questions but thankfully doesn't push for more than the simple stuff. It's too early for my brain to function without caffeine first.

Once satisfied with my answers, she considers the review done and sends me on my way. I walk through the halls and down the steps to the back of the estate. I take the door that leads to the garden and begin the trek to the training area. It's situated further from the estate to accommodate the barracks there. Most of the individuals in Lucifer's army remain there.

We didn't go within the training area yesterday but briefly walked past it so as I enter through the gates. I'm stunned with how much it resembles a small community. There are small shops, bakeries, taverns, and more. I keep moving forward, past all the small shops, toward another stone gate at the end of the main road. I assume it's the training area.

Passing through the stone gates, I feel an energy course through my body. It's strange and I focus on the sensation. I realize its energy saturating the air from all the training. It's fascinating. Unsure of where to go, I reach in for my connection to Kai. I know I may not be his favorite person but at least he'll know where I'm supposed to go.

I let it pull me further into the compound, passing many individuals sparring on mats, running obstacle courses, and conditioning. There are large open fields reminding me of football fields, where several hellhounds of various sizes run and spar. They're beautiful and I can't help but feel curious about how I would look next to them.

Excitement bubbles up in me at the possibilities unfolding just from having access to this training area. I'm distracted by it as I continue to follow that pull to Kai, but I pause as his frowning face stares down at me from where I've bumped into his chest. We're standing at the edge of one of the large training areas set up as an obstacle course with a small group of warriors stretching behind him.

"You're late," he says in greeting, and I smirk, feeling sassy.

"Is that any way to treat a lady this early?" I smile playfully and he growls.

"Don't sass me. Here, I'm your trainer and general. You'll do as I tell you. Do not be late tomorrow." He turns and I move to join the group, smirking. I think I touched a nerve.

The group is made up of two males and two females. The one with blue hair and a pixie cut looks familiar but I can't place where I would have met her. She stretches on the outside of the group but carries on an easy conversation with the others.

As if sensing my gaze, she smiles at me and waves me over. I nod in return and make my way to her.

I plop down and introduce myself. "Hi, I'm Ember." I offer the group a small wave.

She smiles and continues to stretch. "I'm Vixie. Welcome to the group." She turns to the others, "Hey, guys, this is Ember."

They smile and the male furthest from us grins. He's burly with silver hair and red eyes. "I'm Leon. Nice to meet you, Ember."

The male next to him has orange hair and gray skin. I'm fascinated by his appearance and even more so by his neon orange eyes. "Hi, I'm Blaze. Welcome to the pack, Ember."

Finally, the woman next to Vixie, with long burgundy-colored hair, silver eyes, and tan skin, gives me a terse nod before speaking. "I'm Charity. Welcome, Ember."

"It's nice to meet you all," I say and start to stretch.

Vixie whispers to me, "So, I see you're the fabled Lucifer's daughter we've been hearing rumors about. Where have you been hiding for so long?"

I laugh lightly leaning into my stretch. "Honestly, I didn't know I was his daughter until sometime in the last few months. I thought I was a latent shifter."

Vixie nods. "Makes sense. I got my magic late too."

I watch her as she sits up from her stretch and something about her tickles the back of my mind. "Do you know who your parents are?" I can't help but ask.

She looks at me curiously and shrugs. "Yes. My father's dead though. I didn't know him well. My mother's name is Zendaya. She and I don't talk often."

I blink as it all sinks in. Wow, this is her daughter. I can see the resemblance now. She has eyes the color of the sea. "Do you see bits of the future?"

She tilts her head to the side. "Why do you ask?"

I shrug. "Curiosity?"

She lets out a sigh and whispers even softer, "I do but not everyone here knows that. Kai does, but that's because he knows more about me than the others. What made you ask that?"

I look around, eyeing the others, and then whisper back, "I met her, your mother. She helped me escape from Greed. I think you were there, but I didn't see you."

Recognition blooms in her eyes. "You were one of the females he captured?"

I shake my head. "Yes and no. I was there, but I was one of the last to escape. One of the shifters was gifted to some of Greed's generals and I made sure she got out. She's one of my pack members."

"Oh, so that's the big fight that started as I was leading the group north. I wondered what was going on. Wow. Well, I'm glad you got away."

"Alright, group, up we go. Time to train on the obstacles," Kai says loudly, breaking up my conversation with Vixie. "Leon, you start us out. We'll end with Ember."

I watch as Leon stands, shaking his muscular limbs loose. He shoots me a flirtatious smile and takes off to the start of the obstacle course at a jog.

Using his speed, he runs and launches himself to the edge of the giant beam at the start. Large pendulums swing back and forth in an attempt to knock him off. They're padded so as not to hurt too bad, but it still won't be comfortable to be hit. He maneuvers through them easily and does a front flip off the end, landing gracefully before moving to the waterway.

Posts stick out from the water, and he jumps from one to the other while padded arrows fly at him. They must be spelled because I can't see where they're coming from. One gets his shoulder, but he keeps his footing and makes it to the end.

Next, he must climb up a wooden wall with a long rope, roll over the top, and sprint to the finish line. It looks relatively easy until I see someone appear out of thin air.

A massive sword lands in the dirt at the end of the wall and Leon picks it up and moves forward slowly toward the attacker. To finish, he must defeat his opponent.

The figure wears a hood, but I can tell they are watching Leon closely. The two meet with their swords crossed and battle. The clang of the swords echo around us as they spar.

Leon looks as if he'll win until the opponent takes advantage of an opening on Leon's right. He's tagged with the sword but not injured. The opponent throws off their hood and a woman with purple hair, dark skin, and blue eyes smiles at him.

"Return to the line to go again, Leon," Kai declares. "You all have to defeat Tabi in order to pass this obstacle course. Next!"

Blaze goes next followed by Charity and then Vixie. Vixie is impressive as she moves through the course. Her body is fluid, and she makes it look like a dance. I'm impressed, and she smiles at Tabi as she engages her in combat.

The two go at each other hard. Metal clangs and echoes louder than the earlier three. They spin and loop and duck as they move until eventually, Vixie tags Tabi.

"Gotcha!" Vixie cheers and Tabi bows, stepping aside. Vixie quickly climbs the wooden structure, rolls, and lands with a light thud before sprinting to the end.

Nerves hit me as I realize it's my turn. I look at Kai who nods and I make my way to the start. The pendulums are intimidating but I remember dodging the projectiles launched at me by Zendaya and Ulric. They were much faster than any of these course items and unpredictable. All the course projectiles follow a pattern.

Smiling, I watch for the pattern. Seeing it, I launch myself forward. I move through the pendulums easily, cartwheeling off the end. I move across the water without issue as well, dodging the arrows. One comes too close, but I angle myself, balancing my weight on my left foot and shift at the last minute. I feel the wind from it ruffle the hair on my arm.

I reach Tabi and worry floods my brain and my heart rate increases. Can I compete against her? I pick up the sword, feeling its weight in my hands as I move forward. I smile and send up a thankful thought to the training Seth had me do with weapons as I meet Tabi's sword with a sharp jolt.

I can see in her eyes that she's impressed, and we dance around in a circle, meeting each other blow for blow. She laughs as if she's enjoying herself and I ignore it as I focus more. She has got to have a weak spot. It's there somewhere. I need to find it to win this.

I rotate us in the other direction and as I parry her swing, I notice a small give in her hip as she shifts her weight. That's my spot.

I turn her again, keeping her focused on my arms and make my move. I force myself closer and as I do, I push on her hip. It causes her knee to buckle, and she drops to the ground, catching herself with the other leg.

I step back as she pulls herself up. "Well done, Ember. You've obviously had some training. You may pass." Tabi ushers toward the wooden structure. I see the finish line where Vixie waits, beaming, and I quickly finish the last of the course.

Vixie slaps me playfully on the back as I pass. "Great job, girl! That was awesome. I honestly didn't expect you to make it through."

I frown lightly. "Thanks, I guess?"

"Let's watch and see who makes it through next. We normally only get two chances. Those that fail get extra conditioning."

"Oh fun. That's good to know for future sessions." I turn and watch as Leon begins again.

Leon looks irritated as he starts again but this time, he makes it through. Blaze and Charity do as well but barely. The three of them struggled to best Tabi. It almost looked as if Tabi felt bad for them and took it easier, but maybe not.

"Alright, everyone, let's move over to the sparring area. We're going to work more on using a two-handed sword. Partner up!" Kai's voice is loud, echoing around us, and I watch as everyone goes to who I assume is their usual partner. This leaves me alone.

I follow the group as we move to the next area, and we grab swords from a huge rack of weapons. I look at Kai as everyone begins, and he lets out a heavy sigh. He moves to grab one to use himself and walks my way with a frustrated expression on his face.

I shrug as he stops before me. "Sorry. It's not like I had any other options."

He grunts. "I know. Get into position. You've had more training than I expected."

I smile. "I'll take that as a compliment. So, are you going to be stuffy while we spar?"

He moves forward to engage me and I meet his swing. I sense he's holding back. Curious.

"I'm not stuffy. Focused is a better word."

"You are stuffy or is asshole a better word? You could at least try to be nice."

"When have I not been nice? I haven't spoken to you much until now."

"Exactly. Your reaction to who I am is not typical."

His hits increase in strength, and I know I'm edging in on sensitive territory.

"I was surprised. What else did you expect?"

"That was surprise? You were pissed!" Frustration surges and my magic amps my strength up. My hits are harder, and Kai's face becomes stern.

"I wasn't pissed. I don't know you well enough to follow through with the connection. I don't agree that when one finds a mate, they should just accept it." He pushes back against me harder and our speed increases.

I feel power surge through our connection, and I can feel he's angry. My skin heats and I feel my hellhound surface.

"I see. You're pissed because you feel like you weren't given a choice. Newsflash, that's how mates work." I sweep a leg out and he jumps, avoiding it and circles around me.

His voice is deeper and his eyes glow as he moves back in. "Don't preach to me about mates. I've seen enough people pair off over the years. I'm not some young pup."

He jabs toward my side where I previously had an injury that was life threatening. Thanks to Zeke's blood though I healed with some extra rest.

I cartwheel and sail over his sword. I land and swing my leg out, knocking him to the ground and quickly move to pin him with my sword resting under his chin. He reacts quickly and rolls away, spinning and swinging his sword up at me. I spin and block, growling as I do. It pisses me off that I couldn't get him to yield.

His swings and thrusts increase even more in speed and tempo and I see his eyes glow bright. I block as best as I can but I'm no match to the years of training he's had. Eventually, my arms buckle and, in an effort to protect myself, I roll away as the sword falls. Kai pauses with his blade at my chin.

"We're done here," he says with finality in his voice. His chest heaves in frustration and fatigue and I know my body mirrors his. I also can't deny the heat pooling between my legs. That was fucking hot even if he's mad. Wow.

Claps sound off around us and I glance up to see a crowd has gathered to watch us. It's not like we were trying to put on a show. Kai moves his sword away from me and doesn't offer me a hand up. I push myself up from the ground and dust myself off.

"Move to conditioning, group. We'll finish there for the day and meet again in the morning." He glares at me and then turns it on the rest of the group.

I roll my eyes as Kai walks away from me and I move toward Vixie who is starting push-ups. I drop down next to her and do the same.

"So that was impressive. I've never seen anyone take Kai on like that. He also seemed angry," Vixie says, keeping a steady pace.

"So, he's not always uptight?" I lift a brow doing my own push-ups slowly.

"Yes and no. That was different. He's not usually that moody. Maybe Charity quit giving him some, and he's ticked because of that. They've had an on-again off-again thing for a while." Vixie pauses to catch her breath and shrugs.

My heart drops and I feel nauseous. "Do they still have a thing?" I stop doing push-ups and watch Charity as she's doing burpees across the way.

"Like I said, I don't know. Let's go knock out our laps. Kai's not worth trying to get with. He'll never settle." Vixie pushes from the ground.

I follow, pushing up slower. "Noted."

We finish our conditioning and get dismissed for the day. I pause to think about where I'm to go next and remember that I'm to meet someone for training on witchcraft.

I let out a heavy sigh as I make my way back up toward the estate house. My body feels drained, and I can only hope that there will be some food waiting for me in this next session. If not, I'm going to have to start carrying a bag of it around with me.

I walk through the halls and up the stairs to a small room that Arminda pointed out. The door is closed so I knock and listen intently.

"Come on in, Ember," a musical voice responds.

I push the door open and take in the miniature library that's the witch's office. An older woman with dark skin, long gray hair, and silver eyes sits at the back of the room. She has on a long dress and books rest before her as if she's been reading.

"Hello, dear." She stands from her large oak desk. "I'm Minerva. Welcome to your first lesson in witchcraft."

"Hi, it's a pleasure to meet you." I smile and move forward. She pulls me into a hug as I reach out to shake her hand.

"Have a seat there. We'll begin with some breathing exercises and then I'll give you some reading material. We won't do much today but go over the book. We'll begin working spells later. I want to be sure you can focus your mind first for the task. Many struggle with that."

"Oh, you mean like meditation focus? I can do that."

"Good. You will show me. If I approve of your focus, we may try some simple spells. Let's get started."

§

Hours later, after a long and overwhelming day, I drop onto my bed and pull out my compact mirror to call my family. I go through the visualization process and smile as all their faces pop through.

"Hey! I'm so glad to see you guys! How are things?"

My sisters smile up at me and Tansy looks mischievous as she says, "Things are going well. Guess who found their mate early?"

Winnie blushes a scarlet color and my parents roll their eyes. I'm a bit surprised but fate works weirdly.

"Winnie, did you?" I ask curiously.

"First, let me say that it's weird that it slid into place like that. It just was like bam! I couldn't peel my eyes away from him and he was just as stunned." Winnie smiles dreamily.

Tansy interrupts, "You're not going to believe who it is! It's Seth!"

"What! No way?" I ask and the twins giggle.

My dad's stern voice says, "It is. We've all had a sit-down discussion about it. Your sisters also have some other news to tell you."

"Girls, tell her the important news please. Leave the love life for later," my mom chides.

"Mom, my mate is important. It's a once-in-a-lifetime chance. Not everyone gets multiples like Ember. Let me be excited," Winnie says in a whiney voice.

"Yes, let her." Tansy snickers. "Anyway, Em, we've got a new ability! We can use telekinesis now!"

"That's awesome. Wait, why is this all clicking into place?" I feel a moment of dread sink into my stomach. How fast does time move there compared to here?

Winnie frowns and I know what's coming. "Our birthday is tomorrow."

My mom, sensing my inner turmoil, says, "Honey, we know time is different now, but the girls will be eighteen in the morning."

I just stare at them all in the compact, trying to gather my emotions. I'm missing their birthdays. I've missed so much being in Hell the last two times, and it's only been like two days here.

"Don't be sad, sissy. We know you're not missing it on purpose."

Tansy uses my nickname to break my trance.

I rub my forehead. "I know, but it still sucks. I wish I was there. Today was rough."

"Do you want to tell us about it, sweetie?" My mom smiles at me encouragingly and it's almost as if she's here in the room with me.

"Yeah, that may make me feel better." So, I tell them about my day and the sparring session with Kai. I tell them about his mood and how he's not on board still with us being mates. I tell them about the information I learned from Minerva and about the lessons I had this evening with Arminda.

My family chuckles and comments at various times. They offer support and tell me to give Kai time, but it's all so weird. I wish they were here. Maybe it would hurt less not talking to them, but I hated not seeing them when I was a captive before.

I sigh as our conversation begins to dwindle. "Well, I guess I better let you go. I need to do some reading before going to bed. Arminda will have my hide if I don't do it tonight. I have to review with her before training in the morning. I love you all!"

Chapter 9

Days later, after feeling like I've been dragged through the mud, I sit with Minerva, practicing simple spells on healing. For some reason, they've come to me easily, making Minerva smile.

"Good, now ask the plant to sprout flowers," she says, pointing her finger at the small pot. Her long white hair is tucked behind her ear and her silver eyes sparkle.

"Okay," I say, focusing on the plant before me and white light dances around it. Minerva's tan skin seems to glow as it reflects it.

The plant sways momentarily before growing an inch and sprouting a small bud. It then slowly shakes as the bud grows and begins to open. Bright yellow petals fold out and a sunflower comes to life.

"Excellent job, Ember! That looks amazing. Tomorrow, we'll work on healing small wounds with that power. We're going to use this flower now to learn about time and its manipulation. Not many are able to do much with this spell, but I believe you have it in you." Minerva stands from the table and walks over to the bookshelf behind her desk.

We've been practicing magic in her small study with its desk and walls of shelves. One large window looks out onto the garden and lets the odd light of the day in. The door is even made from a bookshelf and appears hidden on this side but from the hall, it's just a typical wooden door.

The table I'm seated at is situated at the back of the room near the window. A small sitting area takes up the center of the room with a spelled firepit in the middle of it. A green fire dances in the pit and casts odd colors on the walls.

She returns to the table and sets the book in front of me. It's dusty and appears ancient. "I am going to send this book with you tonight for further reading but right now, we are going to try to return this plant to a seed." She reaches out and opens the book.

I wring my hands. "Okay, I hope I can do it."

"You can. Let me hear you say it. Manifest that positivity. Be confident," she says as she turns the book around to me.

"I can do this spell. There. Now what do I need to do?"

Minerva smiles and points down to the book. I see a spell written out in a strange language then translated to English next to it.

Time is now,
But now is evermore,
Reverse once more,
Back to the beginning.

I repeat the spell a few times in my head memorizing the short phrases.

"Do you, have it?" Minerva looks at me expectantly.

"Yes." I nod.

"Okay, now repeat the words in the ancient language of the angels with me. It is stronger when used in that form."

We practice together, pronouncing the words in the older language. It makes my tongue feel like lead, but I finally get them after a solid twenty minutes.

"Now move your hands like this, from this side of the plant to the other. Palms open fully and close your fists at the end of the spell." She demonstrates and I repeat the motions.

"Okay, I think I have it!" I smile and begin the chant, moving slowly from one side to the other as I do. I'm fascinated as the plant reverses its growing process and starts to shrink. First the flower closes and disappears into a bud. Then the leaves start to pull in as the entire plant shrinks down into the dirt.

"Retrieve the seed," Minerva instructs and I dig in the dirt until I find it.

"Wow!" I exclaim, holding the small seed in my hand.

"Yes," she says eagerly. "Now to move it forward." She flips the pages and instructs me with the same hand motions, as I repeat the new spell. I sit the seed on the pile of dirt as I chant. I cheer as the plant returns to its flowered state and Minerva beams. "I think you are going to do well with this magic. Take and study this book. I have others on time magic as well. I think that's all for today, dear."

I stand from my chair as does Minerva. She embraces me and I smile as I lean into the hug. "Thank you again for teaching me all of this."

"You're welcome, dear. I'm glad you enjoy it. I haven't had a decent pupil in years, it seems like. Time is such a funny thing."

Her words make me pause. "Was time once different here? Did it flow differently than it does now? I've always wondered why it's so different from how it is back home."

Minerva looks at me curiously and lets out a long sigh. "In fact, my dear, it once was. I assume you've heard about the balance issue we have here in our realm, correct?"

"I have." I nod. "I'm supposed to play a part in fixing it somehow, according to someone who can see bits of the future."

"Really? I didn't realize you would have a role to play with that. Well, the issue with time is a result of a powerful witch seeking personal gain, who lived here ages ago. She sacrificed two weaker witches to change it. She went into hiding after that happened and no one has seen hide nor hair of her since. I believe that the time difference can be fixed with the right amount of power."

"Do you think I could do it?" I meet her wizened gaze with hope.

"It's possible, my dear. We would need another though, with strong power in their veins, most likely like that of the oracle you mentioned."

"What if they have the same blood of said oracle?" I ask, thinking of Vixie.

"Hm, that could work. Study on that book and I'll do some research of my own. If I can find the spell and you can talk your friend into it, we may be able to pull it off."

"I'll talk to her tomorrow. I may be late though since the best time to chat with her is after our training together. Would that be okay?"

Minerva frowns and moves toward the table. She picks up a list of herbs that we have been working on. "It'll be fine if you will memorize this tomorrow and be ready to recite it at our next meeting. This way you're not missing out on anything."

I take the list from her. "I can do that."

"Excellent. Get going before Arminda comes looking."

I nod and sprint toward the door. Hope simmers in my chest as I walk through the halls toward my room. I push open the door and find Arminda sitting at my table, drinking tea.

"Am I late?"

Arminda smiles at me as she rests her cup on the table. "No. I've been enjoying the silence of your room. You also have a better tea stash. I'll have to travel into the small village to get more tomorrow. Would you like to come and see more of the surrounding area?"

I move toward the counter to fix myself a cup of java. Arminda thankfully turned on the pot. "I would love too! Can I invite someone along?"

She looks at me curiously. "Sure. I'm not used to that kind of request though. Who will be joining us?"

I take my cup and sit across from her at the table. "Well, I have a girl that I've been training with that I would like to get to know better. Her mother is a close friend of mine. I'll ask her tomorrow."

Arminda gives me a knowing smile. "You must be talking about Vixie. She's a precious thing. I tutored her for a while myself. I would love for her to join us."

I smile. "Did she ever take any classes with a witch as I'm doing?"

"No, she didn't. Why do you ask?"

"Well, Zendaya, her mother, can do a few things like what Minerva has had me do and I'm curious to see if she'll be able to help me with a certain spell. It's a strong spell and Minerva thinks she may be able to do it."

Arminda nods. "Can you share more about the spell?"

I sip my coffee and look at the books I sat on the table. "Minerva taught me a time spell today. She told me there was a witch that messed up the way time flows between the realms years ago, by sacrificing two weaker witches. She mentioned it could be reversed by stronger witches."

"So, it's an intense time spell? What is needed for said spell?"

"I don't know yet, but we're going to investigate it. I asked her if I could talk to Vixie since her mother has oracle abilities. She said it would do well to have her help." I shrug and sip on my coffee.

"Zendaya has oracle abilities? I never knew that. I would have had Vixie working with a witch had I known that. I'll speak with Lucifer and add her to your classes. Kai might be upset because that will pull her from some of the work she's doing for him, but this seems like a better thing to focus on. Maybe even help with balancing things around here."

"That is exactly what I said, and it should put time in line with earth. I hopefully won't miss so much that way. Did I tell you I missed my sisters' birthdays?" I frown down at my cup.

"You didn't. I'm sorry, Ember. I don't want you to take this wrong when I say this, but you do know you will outlive all your family on earth, right?"

I pull my gaze from my cup to Arminda. "I hadn't thought of that. Oh my gosh. How do I tell them that?" I panic for a moment, and it turns to a deep sadness.

"It's difficult to tell someone. You'll know when the time is right. Let's work on your studies for a bit before you need to meet Lucifer for dinner. It seems like today has put a lot on your plate for you to mull over."

Chapter 10

I arrive early at the training field feeling energized. The smell of my morning coffee seems to linger around me. I begged Arminda to do a short review so that I could speak with Vixie before training, and I won't be too late for classes later. Just as I hoped, there aren't many people here yet, but Vixie is on the field, warming up.

"Hey, Vixie," I say, walking toward her.

She stops her jumping jacks and smiles at me. "Hey, Ember. You're early. Did Arminda give you a break today?"

I shake my head. "No, I wish. She did give me a shorter review though."

Vixie laughs. "She's a tough one."

"Seriously. So, I wanted to ask you something."

Vixie eyes me curiously. "Okay?"

I laugh as she draws out her words. "I was wondering if you wanted to go into the village with Arminda and me today. She has to get a few things and wants to show me around."

Vixie jumps and places her arms around me in a hug. "I would love to go! I haven't gone in so long. It's more fun to go with someone."

I return the hug lightly, having been caught off guard. "I also wanted to ask you another question. This one is a little more serious and I think I need to give you some background first."

She eyes me warily this time. "Okay, but we better stretch as we talk. I see Kai headed our way."

I roll my eyes. "Of course, he's already coming this way. Asshole."

"Hey." She playfully slaps my arm as I sit on the ground. "Don't let him hear you say that. He'll make us run laps."

"Fine. So, I've been working with Minerva on witchcraft, and she taught me something about time yesterday. Apparently, there is a huge spell that will fix the way time flows here and align all the realms, but I need help with it. I was wondering if you would help me."

Vixie looks at me with her mouth agape. "I don't even know where to begin with that stuff. What makes you think I can help?"

"Well, as you know, I was held captive by Greed for a while. What you don't know is that your mother helped break the spell that took my memories. One of my mates also helped in that as well. Anyway, the magic in your blood, is the same magic that she has, and it's powerful."

"Holy shit, that explains a lot. Wow. Okay. So, you really think I can do something like that?" She looks stunned as she waits for an answer. I hear Kai stop a few feet away.

"Yes, I think you can and so does Minerva. I don't know much about the spell yet but she's researching it. Arminda suggested maybe having you take classes with me."

"Holy shit, I'm in. I'll have to rearrange my schedule though." She looks over my shoulder and I turn to see Kai watching us curiously.

"Morning, Kai," I say eagerly and he scowls at me. No one else is around yet so I let myself go and decide to pick at him. "How's your mood today?" Vixie nudges me and I ignore it.

"Fine at the moment. What do you want, Ember?" He crosses his arms across his chest.

"Oh, nothing out of the ordinary. I'm stealing Vixie this afternoon. I hope you don't have anything important for her to work on."

He turns and looks at Vixie. I follow his gaze and she seems to have paled. "What do you need her for?" He turns his gaze back to me.

"I'll get my tasks done before I go, Kai," Vixie adds.

I growl lightly at her. "She's going into town with me. You can come too, you know. It would be nice to have an escort. Maybe you can share more about you? I mean, it would be nice to know."

This elicits a growl from him, and I laugh. "Ember, I told you not to push it. Knock it off."

I feel our connection tingle and my power responds. It reaches across the connection, and something burns. I meet Kai's gaze and it seems heated.

"What?" I ask confused at the sensation, and Kai shakes his head.

"What are you talking about?" Vixie asks and I look over at her noticing Kai walking away.

"Nothing. So, you want to partner up today if we spar?" I focus on Vixie and put whatever that was that happened between Kai and me in the background.

Vixie nods. "That sounds great. You'll be more of a challenge than the guys are. Tough competition is hard to come by."

I laugh. "Well, that's not good. Why is that?"

This time she laughs. "All the guys fear me. They say I hit too hard."

"She does hit too hard. Why are you girls here so early?" Leon's voice startles me, and we turn to watch him as he sits on the ground next to us to stretch.

"You just need to toughen up." She smirks.

"So, is Kai going to let one of us work with you today?" Leon asks, looking me over. His eyes have a heated look and I lift my brow.

"I didn't know he was keeping me from working with anyone. What gives you that impression?" I ask and Leon chuckles.

"He's purposely paired us all up before you arrived for the last several sessions." Leon looks over his shoulder and I follow his gaze. Charity is talking to him, and Blaze is walking in our direction.

"Dick. Don't worry. You guys can spar with me whenever. I hit as hard as Vixie though, I think. She and I are working together today," I say and mentally send Kai, *have you seriously been keeping them from working with me?*

I watch him as the question startles him and Charity rests a hand on his shoulder. He shakes his head and then looks my way. *Maybe?*

You make zero sense. Did you know that? I glare at him, and he ignores me by turning back to Charity.

"Come on, Ember, let's start with hand-to-hand today." Vixie pulls my attention away from Kai and I nod.

"Right." I push up from the ground and we make our way toward one of the padded training mats. It's elevated from the ground around it, so we step up together and square off.

Vixie moves first and I'm impressed with her speed. She moves to punch my side and I move out of the way. We dodge and I laugh loudly which causes her to pause.

"Why are you laughing?" she asks and I double over.

"No wonder the guys say you hit hard! Your strength comes from your angelic side. I recognize it from sparing with Ulric and your mother." I force myself to straighten up as she comes for me again.

She has a smile on her face, and we talk while we move. "Well, in that case, don't hold back because I won't."

"Noted." I smile and we dodge, parry, and basically dance as we spar on the mat. After a solid thirty minutes, we take a break and I look over and see Kai working with Charity.

I frown as I step off the platform, noticing how little clothing she has on. "Does she always spar like that?" I ask Vixie, and she glances over at them as she passes me a bottle of water.

"No. She does that only when she spars with Kai. It's dumb."

I watch as Charity does this weird jiggle thing and swings at Kai. He blocks her swing lightly and is moving slower. "I thought you guys were the stronger hellhounds?"

Vixie sighs. "We are. She, on the other hand, has slept her way to the position. She can be strong when she wants to be but all she really cares about is trying to tame our leader." She rolls her eyes and I feel bees stir in my belly. It makes my blood boil to know someone is trying to tame my mate.

"Well, how about we change that?" I ask and set my water down.

I start walking toward the two as Vixie sputters water behind me. "What are you doing, Ember?"

"You'll see." I say over my shoulder, feeling my power stir to life. If Kai is going to be an ass about me being his mate, then I'm going to have to put my foot down and claim him.

"Hey, Charity, mind if I work with you for a bit?" I ask with a bit too much enthusiasm. Both Charity and Kai pause and look at me.

Charity glances over her shoulder at me and then turns to Kai. Kai nods, and she shrugs in response. "Sure?"

"Great. Let's do some hand-to-hand shall we?"

"Okay," she says and turns to face me. She sets up into her starting stance and Kai moves off the platform.

I smile and then wink at Kai as I advance on his supposed lover. I circle her, making it a game, and I feel my energy spike. My body heats and I go in for a hit.

Charity dodges the first one just barely but misses the second one I had following the first. It snaps her head to the side, and she readjusts with a glare as I back away. I faintly register a snicker that sounds like Vixie off to the right, or maybe not.

Charity tries to hit me, and I block her punch. I swing up with my leg and it flings her sideways with more force than she was prepared for.

She pushes up from the mat. "That was a little hard. Why are you being so rough?"

I smile viciously. "That's what sparring is for, is it not? We need to be prepared for anything. This shouldn't be much different from how Kai hits."

She pouts and comes at me again, trying to move faster. I faint, and it throws her off. She tries to regain her balance after swinging and missing and I take advantage of the situation. With her balance offset, I swing my leg up and roundhouse kick her, causing her to fly into the mat with a thud.

I stand back as she groans in pain and peels herself off the mat. As she stands, she looks at me and I can see her eyes have turned green. Her magic is surfacing. Anger crosses her face, and she begins to shift.

"No, Charity, don't!" Kai yells, but it's too late. She barrels toward me with a snarl.

I smile and let my magic wash over me, letting my hellhound free. I'm bigger than she is and, as she goes to grab me with her jaws, I jump straight up. She sails under me and as I land, I twist around to face her once again.

You can do better than that, Charity, I say, trying to incite her anger even more.

She snarls and I respond with the same. I let her get her teeth into my hide, giving her a sense of empowerment, before rolling us over. She lets go as we do, and I flip over and get her in the shoulder with my jaws.

I taste her blood on my tongue and I release her by stepping back. Her eyes are wild as the pain from my bite hits her. She prepares to launch herself at me again when a wolf larger than me jumps before her. He pushes her down from midair with his paw and holds her there.

That is enough! Kai's deep voice echoes around us.

Charity whimpers beneath him and he lets her up. He turns his burning gaze on me, and I can't help but feel myself swoon over his hellhound form. His muscles are rigid beneath his fur that's as dark as the night sky. His amber eyes seem to bore into mine and my animalistic brain takes over.

Instead of staying back like I should, I saunter up to him and rub on him affectionately. I slide my head against his shoulder, and I feel him stiffen. Charity looks up from her submissive position on the ground and something akin to understanding crosses her furry face. With Kai and I so close together, even though we haven't had sex, it's obvious that our scents are the same. I've successfully made it clear that he's taken and that it's time for her to back off.

Knock it off, Ember. He growls and pushes me lightly. He looks down at Charity. *Take the day off and get yourself checked out. Your wounds need to heal. Everyone else, get back to work. Ember, a word but after we shift back.*

I roll my eyes and let the change wash over me. I put my hands on my hips and watch as he and Charity do the same. Charity shakes herself and gives me a sad look before walking away from the mat.

I cross my arms over my chest as Kai focuses on me. He's pissed and I guess I get it. Something had to give, though.

"What in the hell was that?" He glares at me but moves closer, so our words aren't overheard.

"What do you think it was?" I smile.

"Stop evading the question. Did you plan that?"

I shrug. "Maybe a little. It's not my fault she can't hang with the big dogs."

He runs a hand through his hair. "That was uncalled for. She's worked hard to get a spot on this team."

I tilt my head to the side. "Has she? Are you sure that her vagina isn't the one that worked hard?"

He turns red and I feel slightly panicked. I stand my ground as he says, "You think I've been sleeping with her?"

"Haven't you? All I did was stake my territory. You have a mate now whether you want to accept it or not."

"You have got to be fucking kidding me," he says and grabs my arm. He pulls me toward the back of the training area where an older building sits. I don't fight his hold on my shoulder but glance around curiously as he takes us through a door that leads to a weight room. He glares at the few individuals training there and they immediately leave.

Locking the door behind the last one to leave, he turns his heated gaze on me. I'm stunned because it's not the same look he was giving me two seconds before.

As he prowls toward me, his words set me on fire. "I haven't slept with anyone since I helped save you that night at the gate. Something kept me from doing such a thing even when Charity came to my door, wearing nothing but a thong. When you confirmed what you were to me, my brain went into shock. I put off the idea of ever finding a mate years ago. I got close to one female who was killed in an attempt to break me, and I vowed to never love again. But you show up and shit hits the fan. I can't fucking sleep or think of anything else other than you."

He continues to move toward me and doesn't stop. Instead, he picks me up and lays me back on one of the workout benches. I feel his desire spill over into our connection as he lets his walls down and I gasp. He takes advantage of it and seals his lips to my mouth.

I moan as he pulls my silk pants off and fights to get my top off. It gets hung as he tries to pull it over my wings, and he rips it off.

"Hey," I protest, pulling back from the kiss, "I liked that top."

"You can like another." He presses into me again and I feel his hardened member in his sweats, pushing against me.

I shift slightly on the bench, reaching for his pants and finally get them pulled down. He pulls back to slide them the rest of the way off and I gape at how large he is as he stands before me. I get only a moment before he's on me again. My legs instinctively wrap around his torso as he moves in closer to my sex.

I toss my head back as he teases me with the head of his penis before plunging in. He fills me completely and pauses momentarily. He drags himself in and out slowly before plunging in hard and deep.

"Oh Goddess, Kai. Don't stop," I moan, and he growls in response as he picks up the pace.

I feel our connection burning like a fire between us and I pull him closer to me. As he pushes me over the edge, I bite down on his shoulder, marking him as mine. He groans and tenses. He bites down on my shoulder in return, and I feel myself building again. I groan, still holding on to him as the bond settles completely into place and we climax together.

We release each other and he rests his head on mine as we come down off our high. "I'm sorry I made you wait."

I reach up and push his hair back from his forehead. "It was worth it."

He chuckles deeply and helps me stand. We walk to the back of the weight room to the showers and clean ourselves up. He washes me and I smile as I wash him in return.

Once dressed, we make our way out of the weight room, me wearing just my sports bra and yoga pants. The mark on my shoulder is beginning to heal already. It's nestled where all the other marks have been placed.

Only the ones of my mates remain. Corey's faded shortly after he and I had sex for the last time.

As we walk toward the rest of the group that's still training, they all stop and look at us curiously.

"Did you two just do what I think you did?" Vixie asks as we approach, and I notice Blaze and Leon looking at us with wide eyes.

"Ugh, depends on what you're thinking?" I say and shrug, looking over at Kai.

He rolls his eyes. "Everyone, call it a day. We'll meet again tomorrow."

I tilt my head sideways and look at him. "So does that mean I can take Vixie with me this afternoon?"

He sighs. "Yes, she's free to go but I'm going with you as well."

"Mmhm, you two did just do what I thought you did. It's about time someone tamed him." Vixie snorts and pats me on the shoulder.

Kai growls, and I burst out laughing. "We'll talk more about this later. Let's go get ready."

Vixie lets me pull her away from the platform and I feel Kai's gaze on my back. *I'll see you shortly, mate.*

My insides feel warm as we walk away, and I have a huge smile on my face.

"So, did you know he was your mate? Is that why you two have been weird?" Vixie asks after a time.

"Yes. I found out the night you all helped me escape from Greed. He's one of three. My life's been a confusing mess."

"Well, I'm a good listener. How about you tell me everything?" Vixie pulls me close, smiling from ear to ear.

I laugh loudly. "I will but first let's go by and see Minerva and then have some coffee. Arminda will be waiting on me after."

Chapter 11

Arminda is sitting at my table when we arrive in my room a short time later, sipping on a cup of tea. She looks at us as we enter, and I offer her a kind smile.

"Hey, Arminda, it's good to see you again," Vixie says cheerfully.

"Yes, it is, Vixie. Did Ember speak with you about helping with her spell?" Arminda lifts her brows curiously.

"She did. I agreed to try and we stopped by to see Minerva for a bit," Vixie responds.

"Well, that is great news. Will you also be attending class with her?" Arminda looks at us expectantly.

"She will," I proclaim and move to the coffee pot.

"Vixie, how do you take your coffee?"

"Oh, I'll take a peppermint tea please. I'm not much of a coffee drinker. Just a bit of sugar with that." She smiles.

"On it." I grab a peppermint tea bag from the cabinet and check to see that the water is still hot. I turn the kettle on to heat it up a bit more. It takes only a minute or two before I'm able to pour the water into a cup for her. I bring it over to the table and set it down in front of Vixie where she's talking with Arminda about the weather. She nods in thanks and continues to talk. I watch on in curiosity.

When there is a lull in conversation, I ask, "So, are we ready to go to town?"

Arminda shrugs. "I'm ready if you girls are."

"So, before we go, I might mention that Kai will be joining us." I blush and Vixie chuckles.

"He should be in a better mood at least. Arminda, did you know that he and Ember are mates?" Vixie asks, standing from the table.

"She mentioned it. Did he finally accept it?"

Vixie snorts. "You could call it that. These two had a makeup claiming session after she kicked his old flame's ass."

I cut my eyes at Vixie. "You did not make it seem like an old flame before I kicked her ass."

Vixie shrugs. "I didn't know for sure. You proved that it was in the past. She deserved what she got though."

Arminda chimes in, "Well, at least the claiming is over with, and no one will bother trying to mess with him. Your scents had already mingled, anyway."

A knock on the door interrupts our conversation. "Come in," I say loudly. The door pushes open, and Kai enters, wearing a leather set of armor. He nods at us and walks toward me.

"I see you ladies are ready to go. Shall we?" he asks politely.

"We are. Thank you for joining us," I say cheerily.

"Okay, let's go, ladies. I'll lead the way down. It's somewhat of a walk." Arminda sounds pleased.

We move out of the room and down through the castle to the garden. We keep up easy chatter about training and the different parts of history I've been studying on Hell. Kai adds to the history with memories from several events and Vixie seems fascinated. In what seems like no time at all, a small town catches my eye on the horizon. It's quaint, and the design is like something you would see out of a fairy tale.

The streets are paved with brick and smooth as if magic keeps them flat. The buildings are made of wood and brick and have cheery people moving around in front. I'm excited that the town has electricity. I was worried there wouldn't be electricity for the people, but I was wrong.

What fascinates me the most is the variety of people coming and going. There are different colored demons, partial angels, full angels and more. Seeing the variety fills me with joy. There are so many similarities here to the cultures of earth.

"So where are we going first?" I look to Arminda for direction.

"Oh, can we go to the weapons store first? I would love to go check out what they have. It's been a hot minute since I've been there," Vixie eagerly says.

"I think that would be a great place to go." Kai's deep voice sounds amused.

"Okay, we'll start there and then we'll make our way through the clothing stores. Ember needs something to wear for her introductory party that Lucifer will be hosting soon." Arminda twirls her hand in the air.

"I thought he was going to talk more with me about that before we started planning it?" I frown.

"Well, he informed me this morning to start looking for clothes for you so maybe he's going to speak to you about it more at dinner tonight? I don't know. I just know that I must follow directions when it comes from him." Arminda shrugs.

I roll my eyes. "Fine, but I'm not wearing anything frilly. That's just not me. No offense, Arminda."

Arminda frowns. "While we're here, let's make sure you're fitted for more casual outfits and then I'll get the seamstresses going. I can make sure none of your clothes are frilly as you say. I know some of the dresses in your closet are that and you'll need to wear them for certain events. Does anything you brought from earth need fixing? We could cover that as well."

"I don't think so. I'll let you know when something does."

The group continues forward down the street for several minutes before a large building with a massive sign comes into view with *Weapons* written in bold. There's a huge forge to the side where loud clanging comes from. Steam billows out of the top and people go through the stone doors on the front of the building.

"Wow, that's where we're going?" I ask with my mouth slightly agape.

Vixie squeals. "Yes and while we're there, we need to get you some armor! You don't have any yet, right?"

Kai adds, "She doesn't. That's been on the list Lucifer gave me at the start of the week. We can get her lighter armor here, but Borg is having some stuff brought in from my great-uncle for her war armor."

"Do what now?" I ask, looking between the two. "Can someone explain that in English?"

Vixie laughs. "Basically, you'll need different armor for different occasions. For lighter missions and what not, your leather set will do. It's similar to what Kai has on. For full-out wars, you'll have a special set. I do hope we don't have one anytime soon."

I groan. "That's a lot of armor. Unfortunately, though, we may have a war sooner rather than later. Especially with the way Greed is prepping."

Kai growls, "Don't remind me. That's a sticky area."

I sigh. "Let's go in and get this armor started."

The rest of the afternoon moves by quickly. I am poked, prodded, and fitted to many different outfits and armor. I chat easily with everyone and share bits and pieces of my life. I find out Vixie was raised by her father's grandparents, in the small hellhound training village. Her father disappeared shortly after her arrival.

Kai doesn't open up too much about his life but mentions that his mother is Cerberus' youngest niece. He was raised in a small town not far from the gate Cerberus guards, which is the only gate that leads to Heaven from Hell. His mother and other family members help guard it with Cerberus.

We sit, sipping on beers, in a tavern with our items piled near us. It's relaxing and gives us more time to chat. I people watch as we sit and eventually zone out. This small town is much more peaceful than I expected and makes me feel at home.

It's as I'm watching people that I notice a strange group clustered at the back. The men lean forward and talk in what seems to be a way to not be overheard. They're wrapped up in cloaks, holding large mugs of beer but something about the one in the middle seems familiar.

I tilt my head and tug on my connection to Kai, causing him to pause in his chat with Arminda. "Do you know anyone in that group?"

He turns to look at the men before meeting my gaze. "I don't but they aren't townspeople. They must be traveling through. Not many stop here. Don't worry about it, Ember."

I shrug. "Okay. I get a weird vibe from them though."

"What is a vibe?" Vixie asks. "I've never heard that word before."

I smile. "It's basically an energy. Their energy feels weird."

"That makes sense." She sips at her drink.

"I think we need to head back. Ember, you need to freshen up before dinner later. Tomorrow, we resume your regular schedule, and you have a lot of reading to complete tonight." Arminda pushes up from the table and we follow.

Kai gets the door for us, but I feel eyes on us. I try to ignore it and not worry about it, but something feels off. I glance around and move in closer to my group as we walk. The group of cloaked figures comes out the door a few minutes after we do. They're watching us and I'm getting red flags.

Kai, that group followed us.

I watch as he looks over his shoulder and sees them. One of them branches off and leaves down an alley but the other two follow us, not hiding that they're watching us anymore.

"Gentlemen, can we help you with something?" Kai's words echo around us as he addresses the group and his power pulses through the air, following his words.

I stop and hear Arminda and Vixie do the same. None of us move as Kai takes a step closer to them.

One of the men throws his cloak back to reveal a head of black hair and green eyes. He's smiling eerily. "Just taking a chance to fulfill a request." The man shrugs and his partner lifts an arm and launches something silver toward us. I gasp as Vixie throws a hand up and catches a small dart.

"How dare you threaten us?" Kai growls and charges the pair. He whips his sword out of his sheath as he does, and the two cloaked figures meet him with theirs. Kai locks his sword with theirs and I blink as the sound reverberates within me. I'm not sure what I should do. Do I help him or stay with Arminda and Vixie?

The group is a blur as Kai takes on the two. I continue to struggle with my decision when Vixie's sudden movement beside me catches my eye. She's launched the dart back at one of the men and nails him in his left eye. He drops and his partner pauses, giving Kai the chance to run his sword through him. I stand open mouthed as the second man drops to his knees. Kai pulls his sword out and finishes him off by lopping off his head. The small skirmish is over.

"I'll get someone down here to deal with their bodies," Kai declares, walking toward us as if nothing happened.

I glance around the street and notice no one is around. "What about the people who live here?"

"They won't bother with them. They know not too. This kind of thing happens on occasion. Let's get you all back up to the estate now." Kai sheaths his sword after wiping it with a cloth he pulled from his pocket and motions us forward.

Bewildered, I force myself to move. Why is it so common that the townspeople know what to do without being told? I hope there's a way to change that.

The trek back is slower with all the bags and emotions circulating but we make it in no time at all. Arminda helps me to put my items away. Kai and Vixie leave to put their items up and that's when I realize Kai's room isn't too far down the hall. The realization shocks me and my mind churns out steamy fantasies.

"Ember, are you listening?" Arminda asks, hanging items in my closet while I set my armor up on the stands we purchased.

"No, what did you say?"

"I asked how your essay for me was going on chapters eighteen through twenty-five in *A History of the Realms*?"

"Oh, I'm almost done with it. I have to go over it and check for misspellings and what not, but it'll be done in the morning."

"Excellent. I'm curious to read it. Alright, I'll leave you to get ready for dinner and see you bright and early. Have a good night, dear."

"Thanks, Arminda!" I cheerily respond as she walks out the door.

Once it's closed, I move around the room, changing my clothes and refreshing my hair to look presentable for dinner. Making my way down the hall, I push the door open and stare in surprise as Kai sits next to Lucifer. Lucifer meets my surprised face with a smirk.

"It appears congratulations are necessary. Kai informs me that you completed the mating process. It's about damn time, am I right?" Lucifer slaps his hand on the table and looks at Kai.

"Yes, we did. Um thanks?" I say and make my way toward Kai. I take the seat next to him which is different from my normal spot.

"I've given him the if-you-hurt-my-daughter speech, darling, just so you know. I've never had the chance to do that before. This is all new territory," Lucifer prattles on.

"He did not give me the talk, Ember. Just so we're clear. I'm sorry I haven't joined you both for dinner until now," Kai says, looking remorseful.

"It's okay. I get it. It took you too long to accept me. We'll work past it. Eventually, my other mate will arrive, and you'll have to adjust again. Speaking of which, I need to try and contact them soon. I need updates on what's going on with the pack," I say and grab for the glass of water in front of me.

Food is brought in as Kai asks, "Why do you worry so much about it? Can they not handle it?"

I swallow my drink as food is placed before me. "I'm sure they can but it wouldn't be successful. Alpha Gale has recruited the help of a dark witch. I've been curious if it's the one Minerva talked about messing up time. I don't want any of them to get hurt while taking Alpha Gale down."

"If it is her, then you have my permission to use whatever you need from our estate here to help," Lucifer adds and I gape at him.

"Are you sure?" I ask incredulously.

"Of course. It isn't only mine to control and command anymore. It may help to include other strong witches such as Minerva. There are others that live in town who I'm sure can help if needed. It may take some convincing though if it is Katara." Lucifer reaches for his fork.

"I'll do whatever you need me to do, Ember. If we have to go topside to take someone down, our group will go. Speaking of which, Charity requested to be moved to a different group after the events of this morning. I thought you would like to know." Kai gives me a stern look and I blush.

"What happened this morning?" Lucifer looks at us curiously and I blush even more.

"Ember took it upon herself to kick Charity's ass because she assumed we were still sleeping together. She didn't know I haven't been able to touch another female since we met." Kai shrugs and Lucifer bursts out laughing.

"That a girl! You do have a little of me in you after all. Well, Charity will be fine. Will you add another to the group?" Lucifer asks cheerfully.

"In time, yes. The right person will come along." Kai begins to eat his food and I feel my blush ease away.

"You two are so odd sometimes," I say as I pick up my fork.

The rest of dinner goes by easily with casual conversation. We share the event at the tavern which causes some concern, but it's apparently nothing new. Lucifer is more at ease with Kai present, and it makes me relax even more around him. Conversation doesn't feel as stiff as it has felt as of late.

Once finished, Kai walks with me down the hall. "Would you like to come to my room, Ember?" He gives me a pleading look.

"Sure." I smile, and he leads me past my room to a door further down.

He pushes the wooden entry open and leads me into a room filled with warm colors. Golds, reds, and whites, make the room feel comfortable and homey. Dark brown furniture that's worn from years of use decorates it with occasional abstract art scattered throughout.

"I'm not the best at decorating but these colors have always called to me. The paintings were gifts given to me from helping those in need, over the years," Kai says as I walk toward one resting over an empty fireplace.

Blues, purples, oranges, and yellows in various shapes create an abstract of a sunset. "This is so pretty. True art is always better than the stuff sold at department stores."

Kai looks confused for a moment before shrugging it off. He pulls me toward his bedroom. I faintly register that his rooms are laid out like mine. I take in his four-poster bed as we stand in his room with maroon blankets. There are red accent pillows and the whole combination makes me think of red wine.

I squeal as he picks me up and carries me to the bed. Lying me gently on it, he leans in and seals his lips to mine. Heat sparks in my blood and my body aches for him. His erection rubs against my legs, and I move them, wrapping them around his torso, and pull him in closer. He groans as I grind into him and he pulls back enough to remove my top. He slips it over my head and that's when I notice how soft his bed feels. "Is this silk?" My brain blurts out, and he looks at me with a lifted brow.

"They are. Is that important right now?"

I shake my head. "Nope." I grab him and pull him into me.

He reaches around and braces himself on the bed as he steadies himself above me. I feel him slide his hand under my back to pull up my bra. It lifts from my skin easily and he pauses briefly to admire my breasts. I guess he's a boobs guy?

I use his moment of distraction to pull his shirt off. He grunts as it snags when I try to pull it over his head and smiles once he's free of it. I immediately move to tug off his pants and he helps me but frowns down at me since mine are still on. I shrug and lie back as he pulls mine off. We both take each other in. His body reminds me of something an artist would have carved into stone. Like those old Greek statues seen in museums and history books. It makes it easy to forget that he's centuries old.

He urges me to slide further onto the bed and I move up enough to rest my head on the pillows. They too are soft, and I look forward to snuggling into them. Kai grabs my legs and pulls me close. Holding them still on the bed, I gasp as Kai licks my sex, pulling my thoughts away from the soft pillows. Moaning, I reach down and grab his hair, pulling him in closer.

"Oh, that feels good," I groan out and I feel him nip the inside of my lip. The sensation resulting from it has me spiraling off the edge as if a tidal wave has moved through me.

He chuckles, sending vibrations coursing through my sex, once again pushing me near the edge and inserts his fingers. Pumping them back and forth, I grip the sheets around me as he pulls me over again.

"Holy fuck, Kai."

"I think you need one more." He leans in and licks slowly up my center as he gently strokes me on the inside. He reaches up with his other hand to play with my nipple as he continues his wonderful onslaught on my pussy.

"Come again for me," he demands, and I feel my core tightening once more.

"Holy hell," I groan and tip over the edge.

Panting, I look up at him as he pulls away from me and repositions. He lines his member up before gently entering me. I can tell I'm sore from our tryst earlier but the fullness of him seated within me is amazing.

He moves gently in and out while continuing to tweak my nipples. He leans in to kiss me, and in the momentary distraction of his heated lips on mine, I feel his pace speed up. He slides his hand down to my waist, holding me steady as I squirm. In an effort to hold myself at bay from climaxing quickly, I bite into his shoulder. Turns out that was not the best idea. As I feel him nearing his climax, I let go. I scream his name as I plummet for the final time with him.

He holds me as he pulses within me, filling me. I lean into him and focus on controlling my breath. Our bodies are sweaty after our lovemaking, and I blink up at him, unsure what to do next.

"Shower?" he asks, sliding from between my legs and pressing his discarded shirt against me.

"That sounds great."

I slide from the bed and follow him into his en suite bathroom. It's decked out in matching colors to the rest of his rooms with warm brown tiles adorning the shower.

I watch as he turns on the water and it begins to steam. Tossing his shirt to the side, I step into the falling water and let out a contented sigh. It feels like heaven as it hits my skin and I close my eyes, soaking it in.

A moment later, I hear Kai enter through the glass door and open my eyes as he wraps me in his arms. He pulls me close and kisses my lips softly. We remain like this in silence for several minutes before he grabs the soap, and we take turns cleaning up.

Once finished, he walks me to the bed, still wrapped in his towel, and we slide beneath the sheets together. I inwardly do a happy dance, knowing I finally get to spend a night with my third mate. Maybe soon, I'll have them all with me again. Hopefully Ulric is okay and we're able to find him so it can happen.

Chapter 12

Vixie and I sit with Minerva in her small office days later, studying the book about time. Vixie has picked up things as well as I did thankfully, but studying the list and the amount of focus needed for the time spell is exhausting.

The spell itself requires a vast amount of meditation beforehand and then we must find an open area to perform it. Thankfully, Minerva has promised to walk us through it but finding the best time to perform it is troublesome.

"According to this section and based on the calendar over there," I say, pointing at Minerva's wall. "The best time to do this spell would be tomorrow. Is that even doable? Is it too soon?"

Minerva gives me a studious look and then looks at Vixie. "Do you both feel you could tackle such a challenging spell so soon?"

Vixie shrugs. "It's worth a try. You'll walk us through it all, right? It shouldn't be over the top if our energy holds out, right?"

"Correct," she says, eyeing us and looking at the book. "I think I have most of these ingredients already. I know that I have an hourglass somewhere that would work perfectly. It was a gift from an old friend years ago. I hate to part with it, but I think it's for a good cause."

"Can we not search for another one?" I ask, looking at the list of items for the spell again.

"I'm afraid not. No one in town makes them. This gift came from earth. Maybe this was its purpose and why my friend gave it to me. The universe does work in strange ways." Minerva shrugs.

Vixie frowns. "So to do this spell, we need to meditate for an hour, soak in a salt bath with a quartz crystal, and then meditate again before doing the spell? We can't skip some of the meditating?"

I look down at the book. "Do we want to jeopardize it by not following the directions? I'd rather not risk it."

"Ember is thinking cautiously. It's best to do as it instructs. The spell will be difficult enough." Minerva nods. "How are the spells for lighting candles coming?" She looks between us and then reaches for the box of candles behind her on the shelf. "I'm hoping you two have it down since we've moved on to attempting more challenging things."

"I think I've finally got the hang of it. I only set my comforter on fire once while practicing." Vixie twirls her hand triumphantly as Minerva places the candles in a line before us.

"Good. We'll take turns lighting and extinguishing them but this time, I want you to only use your will. No spoken words. Clear your mind and make it happen." She smiles confidently at us.

Butterflies dance in my belly and my palms grow sweaty as I stare at the candles. "Are you sure we can manage that?"

"I believe in you ladies. You've accomplished so much already in such a short time. Try it. Ember, you go first." Minerva waves toward me with a flick of her wrist and I let out a sigh.

I stare at the candles before me and target one. It has a small chip out of its side. Clearing my mind, I force my thoughts toward it and imagine a flame licking up its wick, sending a small tendril of smoke into the sky. After a couple of seconds, my mental image becomes reality.

"Yes! I did it." I jump around in a circle, fist pumping the air, and then turn to Vixie. "Your turn. You've got this."

Vixie focuses on the candles just as I did. I can't tell which one she's picked to light but seconds later, a second flame dances to life and we both cheer.

"Great job, ladies. Now put them out," Minerva says and points at the candles.

Vixie and I both go still as we focus, and I clear my mind. I visualize the flame dimming until it disappears, and it does exactly as I ask moments later. Vixie does the same as well and we both look at Minerva who smiles back with a challenge in her eyes.

"Now each of you will light them all then extinguish them. Ember, you first. Clear your mind and focus," Minerva voices.

I stare at the line of candles, momentarily panicked before taking a few deep breaths. My heart rate slows, and I relax my hands. Feeling calmer, I focus on lighting the candles. It takes a bit longer but after a minute of focusing, they all light at once. I blink and then look at Minerva. She nods and I know it's time to put them out.

This time, I stare at the candles, push my will into the world, and wait. A minute ticks by and then a second one before they go out. I sigh, feeling accomplished but also slightly fatigued.

Vixie goes next, and it takes her even longer, but she manages to light then extinguish them all. We both collapse back into our chairs once it's done and Minerva laughs.

"I'll grab us some tea and some snacks. You can rest right here. Magic can be tiring at times, especially with performing new things. This will feel like nothing compared to how tired you'll be following the time spell."

I gape at her and then turn to Vixie who frowns. "Well, I guess it'll be worth it in the end, right?" I look at Minerva and she pauses at the door.

"I believe it will be, yes." She smiles and exits.

I turn to Vixie. "I didn't think I would be able to do that."

"Me either, but I'm glad we did. Spell work is hard. I think I'd take training in the barracks over this any day. I feel a headache coming on."

"I feel you. Mine is throbbing. Maybe the food and tea will help. I sure hope so." I grab her hand and give it a squeeze.

We stay relaxed in our chairs until Minerva returns. She gives us both a plate filled with a sandwich, chips, and a pickle then rests the tray with cups and a teapot on her desk. She fills our cups, and we sit in silence as we drink and eat.

"I think tomorrow will be a good time. You ladies can handle it. I believe in you. No training in the morning though. I'll speak with Kai. Save your energy for the spell." Minerva waves her hand across our mostly empty plates, and they refill.

I stare in awe before picking up the food that appeared. It doesn't taste any different from what was there before. Shrugging, I continue to eat, letting my thoughts drift to the spell work we'll be performing tomorrow.

§

Vixie and I follow Minerva as she leads us from the castle. Each of us carries bags with various things such as candles, herbs, an enormous hourglass, and the book with all the time spells in it.

Humidity weighs heavily around us and the strange sun is hot, as we leave through the garden toward the mountains behind the estate. Morning came quickly, and it was difficult not to fall asleep while meditating.

We pass the shimmering gate that led me here from earth and continue following a small trail leading toward the peak of one of the mountains. It reminds me of a deer trail I followed as a young kid—small and hardly visible.

I remain silent with Vixie behind me as Minerva picks her way over the rocks in front of me. It surprises me how well she moves over the terrain for her age. The trail isn't an easy one to walk and we move along the edge of a cliff the higher we go.

Eventually, we reach a flat space overlooking Lucifer's estate. I notice now that it sits in more of a valley with the small town than what I originally thought. I make a mental note to one day take a picture from this height.

"Alright, girls, we're here. Vixie, I need the salt from your bag to begin making our circle. We'll set everything up once we're in it," Minerva says, turning to face us.

"Right." Vixie nods and reaches into her large bag. She pulls out a massive jar filled to the top with salt.

Minerva takes it from her gently. "I want you two to remain here as I pour the salt. You can empty your bags so that you can find things easier while I do it."

Vixie and I plop ourselves down next to each other in the tall grass, as Minerva moves away, and we empty our bags. We group our items and arrange the candles as we watch Minerva make her way around us forming the circle.

Magic hums in the air as she completes it and bows her head. It smells of moist earth and lavender. Lifting her head, she returns to us in the center and picks up the candles.

"I need you to take these candles and begin lining the circle. Spread some of the cinnamon and mixed herbs with them. It will create another barrier of protection. The big teal candle, I will place with us in the middle," Minerva instructs, and we both jump to our feet.

"I'll start on this side, Vixie," I say, pointing to the right side of the circle. She nods in response.

I sit a candle down and begin to drop bits of the herbs as requested between it and the next candle. I continue this routine until I meet Vixie. We place the last bit of our herbs down and return to Minerva in the middle. She has the hourglass placed next to the teal candle and the book open.

"Okay, use the spell I taught you both to light the candles. Push your will into the spell. Each of you do half of the circle, quickly." Minerva smiles and Vixie and I do as she asks.

I close my eyes and imagine the candles lighting, pushing my will out into the universe. I recall the spell and list it in my head. It no longer feels necessary though. At the sound of a light hiss, I open my eyes and see the candles dancing with flames around us. Vixie has a triumphant smile on her face.

"Okay, ladies, now group up with me. I will light this candle and then we'll begin the spell." Minerva reaches for our hands, and we grasp hers tightly in return.

The teal candle between us ignites and a blue flame dances to life. It's beautiful and memorizing as we stand around it. Magic tingles in my veins as I sense Minerva preparing to start the spell.

"Past, present, and future,
Maiden, Mother, Crone,
Correct that which has been broken,
Align the times in all the realms,
Fix the clock,
Maiden, Mother, Crone,
Hear our plea,
Let the sun rise,
And set once more,
In accordance with thee.
Bind and bound time is now,
So, mote it be."

Magic funnels through us like fire and blue flames erupt around us in the circle. The hourglass shines teal and explodes. As the glass falls around us, the world begins to spin. Everything turns blue and I hold tightly to the women on either side of me. The ground shudders beneath us and as the flames begin to die, we weaken.

Fatigue presses on me as the flames turn into blue lights. They fill the circle around us like flying lightning bugs. It reminds me of my childhood and my many attempts to fill jars with their wondrous light.

"It is finished," Minerva says and each of us drops our hold. Our bodies sag to the ground as we remain at the center of our circle.

"That took a lot of my energy," Vixie says and then yawns.

"Yeah, it did," I agree.

"I knew it would. Less powerful beings would have died. Thank you both for helping with this. Ember, our time should now be aligned with that on earth. Hopefully, that will help with things." Minerva repositions on the ground and pulls her bag to her lap. She whips out smaller bags of ham, cheese, and bread as well as a few bottles of water.

"Thank you, Minerva. I'm curious to see the results when I call my family next. I hope to do that when we get back. Also, thank you for bringing food. Are we going to rest awhile before we go back?" I stretch then reach for some of the food.

"Only long enough to eat and regain some strength. You'll still be weak from doing the spell. By the next day, it'll be a little better, but you'll still be tired." Minerva bites into a piece of the bread.

"That sounds like a wonderful idea. A day off from training is a rare thing, anyway," Vixie adds before biting into some of the cheese.

We sit in silence, chewing our food, as the blue fireflies dance around us. They're magnificent to behold and I feel my energy picking up a little. I don't want to forget the effect of the spell but soon Minerva stands and opens the circle again.

We take our time returning to the castle and Kai meets us as we reach the garden.

"Were you all successful?" He looks to Minerva for confirmation.

She nods. "We were. The girls will need tomorrow off to recover. It sapped a lot of our strength."

Kai nods and thankfully doesn't argue. "That's fine. Ember, may I escort you up to your room?"

I look at him and smile. I feel something simmering in our bond. "Yes. Vixie, Minerva, I'll see you in a day. Have a good rest of the night."

Vixie gives me a knowing look. "Right. Goodnight." She turns to head toward the training barracks where her room is.

Minerva offers me a silent nod before entering the castle. She has a room not far from the small office we use for our classes.

"Did you have something in mind when you came up with this idea?" I ask Kai as we step through the wooden door into the castle.

"I did. I was hoping that I could spend more time with you in your room now that we're mated and all. Staying down the hall from you in my own room has been odd. I don't want that space between us anymore. I mean, we could stay in my room too if you prefer. I have lived there for centuries. But only if you're comfortable with it." He seems unsure as he gets the last of his words out.

"Hmm, I'll think about it. For tonight though, let's go to my room. I'm exhausted."

"I bet you are. I felt the ground shudder here. Did it shudder when you worked the spell?"

"It did. It was amazing and a tad scary." I grab his hand and I tell him about the spell and all the blue fire and light it caused.

When we make it into my room, he kisses me gently and walks me to the bed. He undresses me slowly. Having his hands on my skin seems to relax me even more. Once my clothes have been completely removed, he lays me on the thick mattress naked.

"Do you feel up to it?" he asks, starting to remove his clothes. I don't miss the bulge in his pants before he slides them down.

"I want to, Kai, I really do, but I don't have the energy. Let me rest some and maybe I'll feel better at dawn. You're always so much fun at that time of day, anyway."

He rolls his eyes and chuckles softly before climbing into the bed. He drops down next to me on his side and pulls me close. "Get some rest, mate. You're going to need it. I may take the day off with you tomorrow."

I smile as I snuggle into him and close my eyes. I may not rest as much as Minerva would like me too after all. I mean, I will rest some, but oh to spend all day in bed with him. Hm.

Chapter 13

The following morning, I wake to a light tickle in my mind before Zeke's emotions spill through with his words. *I've come through one of the gates and I'm headed toward my kingdom. I hope to have news for you soon regarding my brother and Ulric.*

I smile at the ceiling with Kai's arm wrapped around me and send him a response. *That's good to hear. How is everyone back home? Are they safe? How are things with the council?*

When I left, they were fine. Seth and your sister are cozy now and he won't hardly leave her side.

Oh jeez, I can only imagine what that's like. I'm planning to call them today. I wanted to last night, but I was exhausted. We did something big.

Oh yeah? Anything you would like to share?

Yes, I did my very first huge spell with Vixie and Minerva. We fixed time between all the realms.

Holy cow, you mean you balanced it all?

Yes, or at least I think we fixed it. I'm going to find out today. I plan to contact everyone back in the pack through the mirror and see what time it is there and then compare it to our time. I'm hoping that maybe it corrected itself.

That's excellent.

Does it take long to reach home now that you're through the gate? I wiggle next to Kai, trying to stretch out some.

No, just a few hours if I run the whole way. Nothing too big. Maybe you can come visit my kingdom soon since you're officially in Hell.

I smile to myself. *I'd like that.*

Well, you could come sooner rather than later. Maybe you could talk to your little group of friends into coming with you. That way you're protected on the way here and they would be our guests.

You know, that's not a bad idea. I'll talk to Kai about it today and see what he thinks. I do want to talk to my parents first to see how things are there before I plan to travel.

Understandable. I'll check back in later. I feel our connection is stronger now that I'm within the same realm. Weird how that works.

Yes, it is. I love you, Zeke.

I love you too, Ember. I'll see you soon.

Zeke's words drift off and Kai surprises me by saying, "You two are loud. You know, you could have given me a heads-up that you guys were going to talk. I think I would be okay not being included in that conversation. I was sleeping well. You probably should have put your barriers up."

I laugh and he leans his head down onto my shoulder then pulls me closer. "Sorry, eventually I'll remember to get you all into a single blocked section where I can talk to you individually. I didn't even think about doing it this morning. He surprised me. I'm glad he's in Hell though." I laugh again. "That sounds weird coming from my mouth."

"Why do you say that?"

"I could see how it wouldn't faze you, having been here all of your life, but saying that you're glad someone is in Hell isn't exactly a good thing on earth."

"Well, now you have a different view of it and it's not bad. Hell's just a different version of the world you came from with stronger, more powerful beings." Kai shrugs his shoulders, moving us both in the process.

"True."

"I heard the part about possibly visiting Zeke's kingdom by the way. I'll have to run that by Lucifer before we decide to go. You want me to stick around while you call your family?"

"That is completely up to you. I'm not supposed to be doing anything today but resting." I push into sitting and swing my legs over the side of the bed. My body feels heavy with fatigue even after sleeping most of the night.

"Right, but I totally had different ideas for your rest. I'll go get us some food while you call your family. If you're still on the line with them when I come back maybe I can join in the conversation. I don't know. We'll see." Kai slides from the bed and grabs his clothes from the floor.

"I like that idea and I also like the idea of food. I'm starving."

Kai chuckles. "You're always starving but then again, that spell you worked last night took a lot of energy. I'll be back. You stay right here. I even recommend sliding back into bed. Breakfast in bed for a relaxing day."

I smile and flop back on the bed as Kai finishes dressing. He tosses me a t-shirt, and in no time, he slips out of the door, leaving me to my own devices.

Rolling over, I reach to my side table and open the drawer, pulling out the small compact mirror I have there. It's a safer spot in the drawer while I sleep. I empty my head of any thoughts lingering. Opening it, I focus on reaching my family. I feel the mirror warm in my hands.

I am hopeful and exhilarated at what I accomplished yesterday as the mirror fogs slightly. Instead of all the family's faces coming into focus, I see only my parents. Both appear sad, and my mother has mascara running down her face.

"What's wrong?" I ask immediately, feeling adrenaline kicking into my system. My heart rate increases, and I feel ready to fight.

My mother sobs loudly and my father speaks, his voice heavy and deep, "Someone took Winnie and Tansy. The attack happened shortly after Zeke left. I guess they thought we would be weaker once he was gone. Seth is greatly injured and so are Corey and Adam."

"Holy fuck! Who took them? Where are they? I'll kill them!" My anger surges and I feel flames sprout along my arms. My hellhound wants to surface and tear someone's face off.

"I don't know where they went, but a message was left for you from some angel seeking retribution for a female stolen and his missing brothers. I don't know what the note means, but I thought you could make sense out of it." My father's words are stern, and I can tell he's worried and angry with me.

"Well fuck, stupid triplets! I'll hunt that motherfucker down and kill him. I'll drape his insides over his head and let the buzzards eat him. Don't worry, Mom, Dad, I'll find them. I'll fix this and we'll never have to deal with this again."

"Are you sure you can do this? I don't want you getting hurt either. You're all my babies. Can someone else not do it? I know you're the only one who can do it, especially if they're in Hell, but I don't like it." I can see my mom wringing her hands in concern.

"Mom, I can handle this. I have a group of hellhounds that I'm working with. I know we'll be able to get them and bring them back," I growl.

My mom stills. "I believe you, honey. The boys should contact you soon. I think they'll be better in a day or so. Alpha Gale had a special healer come in from what I've heard. She's a very powerful witch."

I frown, staring at the compact, wondering if it's who I think it is. I ask, "Does she have a name? Do you know it by chance?"

Tears spill from my mother's eyes as she speaks. "I don't, but I can find out when I go check on the boys. We look forward to hearing from you soon. Let me know what your group says. We love you, honey. Stay safe."

"I love you both very much. I'll call soon and I'll speak with Kai. We'll get something going. Bye."

I set the compact down and begin rubbing my forehead in frustration. I have no idea how I'm going to go about this, but I need to figure something out. I must save my sisters. There's no way that I'm going to leave them to be tortured by that asshole, especially not after what he did to Amber.

Kai enters the room with a silver tray topped with drinks and food. He takes in my mood and my expression. Then he sees the scorch marks on the bed from my flames that have now disappeared. "What's wrong?"

I look at him sadly, feeling tears threatening to escape. "My sisters were kidnapped. I think Stole did it, one of Greed's generals. He had a bone to pick with me because I rescued the woman pregnant with his brother's baby. She was a gift to them from Greed.

"Shit. What do you want to do?"

"I was going to ask you that. You're one of the leaders here. Do you think my father will approve of us taking a group out to find them?"

"I'm sure we can get it approved. Your family is now my family, and, in a way, an extension of Lucifer's."

"Are you sure?"

"I'm mostly sure. Now let's eat. You're going to need your strength. You're exhausted from yesterday and this may be a challenge. One that you didn't foresee coming.

"Okay." I frown, wiping at my eyes. "Let's eat and then I'll go talk to my father."

He sets the tray down and moves back into the bed with me. We eat a delicious meal of pancakes, bacon, eggs, orange juice, toast, milk, and all kinds of extra goodies. It's almost as if the cooks knew we were going to have breakfast in bed.

After we finish, I force my tired body out of bed and dress. With the time of day, I'll find Lucifer most likely in his office or in the main throne room.

Kai kisses me before he leaves, and I follow him into the hall. I take my time following the halls as I walk toward Lucifer's throne room. My feet pad on the soft carpet, making a light thud as I move.

With nervous butterflies flitting in my stomach, I push the small door that opens behind his throne and enter hesitantly. A line of people waits before him, and several move their gaze over to me as I approach. A murmur fills the room as I continue to approach and Lucifer pauses discussing something with a male standing before the throne.

"Good morning, Ember, is everything okay?" He has a look of concern on his face, and I glance at the crowd before him.

"Can I speak with you privately for a moment?" I question.

He stands and moves from the throne closer to me. He flicks his wrist and a small bubble, visible only by the light shimmer around us, creates a small area of privacy.

"No one can hear us in here. What's wrong? You look troubled."

"Well, I'm a little upset. I got news this morning that my twin sisters were kidnapped. I wanted to speak with you about taking Kai and a group of the hellhounds to find them. I also wanted to meet up with Zeke at the vampire palace and have them aid us as well."

Lucifer frowns at my words. "I want to tell you yes, but I would rather send out scouts first. It'll be a safer avenue to pursue. With you being my only heir, I can't put you in danger. Your introduction to all the upper members of Hell is next week. Let's get past that first and see what the scouts bring back before you go hunting."

"I like the scout idea but is that really important in a time like this? I need to find my sisters." I scowl.

Lucifer scowls right back. "You'll follow my instructions on this, daughter. I'll not lose another heir to those seeking to overthrow me. Plus, the person who kidnapped them may be at the party. What better way to lure them out?"

I growl in frustration, but his words make sense. "Fine, but if we have information on where they may be before the party, then I'll leave immediately following, and take my group with me. Will you be inviting the vampires to said event?"

He nods. "I will. One of your mates is a prince of theirs, is he not? I'll have Ragnar finish sending out the invitations today."

I frown but nod in understanding. I look back at the crowd watching us curiously. "Do they know who I am?"

He shakes his head. "They do not, and it will stay that way until after the party. I'll have you do a formal introduction the following day if you do not leave to find your sisters. If you do leave, I'll send out a formal announcement."

I watch as Lucifer twists his wrist in a circle and the bubble around us drops away with a light whooshing sound. The crowd continues to eye us curiously, but I turn away and head back toward the door I first came through. Lucifer returns to his chair.

As I walk back through the halls toward my room, my heart moves into my throat. I want to cry but I fight the urge to lose myself in my emotions and turn toward the path leading me to the barracks.

I've never been to Vixie's room before, but I enter the barracks through its wooden door and make my way down their stone floors. I stop and ask someone in the hall which one is hers and they point to the end where a worn door remains closed. It has a small blue circle on the outside.

I knock on her door and hear a grumble on the other side that sounds like something akin to enter.

I push open the door and take in her small quarters decorated in shades of blues, whites, and occasional pops of orange. It seems to fit her personality.

"Hey, Vixie," I announce, closing the door behind me. I spy her curled up in her bed beneath a white blanket.

"Why are you here so early? We're supposed to be resting today." She sits up, pushing her wild hair out of her face.

"I know and I didn't plan on resting too much. Kai was going to spend the day with me, but I got news this morning that my sisters were taken."

Her eyes go wide. "When?"

"Yesterday from what my parents said. I want to search for them now, but Lucifer denied me. He wants to send out scouts. I don't know when he's planning to do it, but I don't want to sit still. He wants to wait until after my coming-out party next week to let me go hunt."

"Well, you know I'll go with you. Which scouts is he sending? Did he say? Have you talked to Kai yet about the scouts?" She starts rapidly firing questions. "Do you have a plan on where to start looking? Who could have taken them?"

"Slow down. I have an idea. It's one of Greed's generals, Stole, I believe, who may have done it. I helped play a role in his brothers' deaths and took my friend back from them. She was carrying his brother's child. He's holding a grudge against me. I've no idea where he would be hiding though." I pace side to side in front of her bed.

"Well, we should go over to Kai's office, see who is going to be scouting, and map out where to start. The party will be here and over quickly. Honestly, it's smart to send them out first. You are the only heir." I roll my eyes at her words, but Vixie continues speaking as she crawls out of the bed. "We might also see if Minerva has a spell that can help. Of course, we may not be able to do it until tomorrow, depending on how much energy it needs."

"Your brain is working much faster than mine right now. I'm still reeling from the news that they were taken." I scratch my head as I stop in the middle of the room.

"I've always found that making a plan helps me focus on what needs to be done," she says over her shoulder as she changes into a different outfit.

"I guess you're right." I stand, twisting my hands together as she finishes dressing.

"Let's go find your mate and work our way from there. We'll get a plan of action with the best scouts. Lucifer may be our king, but he doesn't know who will get the job done right. Kai and I do, and we'll make sure we get the right ones on the job."

Vixie motions for me to follow her after she finishes dressing, and we make our way out to the training field where Kai is working with Blaze and Leon. They're doing drills and they all pause as we approach.

Kai looks at me with concern. "I take it Lucifer didn't agree to your plans?"

I frown. "He didn't necessarily deny it. He wants to wait to send me out until more information comes in. The ball is next week, and he wants to be sure that I'm safe. So, he wants to send scouts out first before we go."

Kai nods. "I mean, that's not a bad idea. I would rather know more going in anyway then being sent on a wild goose chase."

"That's what I was thinking," Vixie adds.

"What's going on?" Blaze asks, interrupting us.

I turn and focus my gaze on him and Leon as they watch us curiously. "My sisters were kidnapped. I think it's a way of retribution because I played a major role in the deaths of two of Greed's major generals, the triplets. Stole is the only one that remains alive, and I think he's behind it."

Leon lifts his brow. "Are you positive he's behind it?"

I shake my head. "I don't have proof, but a gut feeling tells me it's him."

"So, what's the plan then? Are we going to get them back?" Blaze asks.

Kai grunts. "I was going to talk to you all about it, but we need to send out the scouts first. I think we should send out our best scouts and plan with what they bring back."

Leon chuckles. "You're going to send out the twins, Marley and Mikai?"

Kai nods. "Of course. They're the best. I don't think they're on any assignments that I can recall right now."

Vixie adds, "The twins are a bit scary, but they move like ghosts and always get the job done."

"So, you all recommend them then?" I ask, glancing around the group that has now created a small circle.

"Yes, they won't let us down and then we can go and find your sisters." Blaze smiles and pats my shoulder affectionately. It elicits a soft growl from Kai.

I laugh as Blaze holds his hands up. "I didn't mean anything by that touch, man. Just to offer comfort."

Kai cuts his eyes at him before looking back at me. "You and Vixie go get the rest you need. I'll get the scouts out today."

I move toward Kai and wrap my arms around him. "Thank you. I'm going to go back to my room and speak with Zeke. We also can't travel there so he's going to have to come to us."

Kai pulls out of the hug. "That's fair. You're the only heir, so Lucifer is being extra cautious. I'll see you soon."

Vixie grabs my hand, and we make our way back toward the estate. I let her lead me, thinking over and over if there is something else I can do to make this process move faster.

"Stop fretting. We'll find them. I'm taking you to your room and we can hang out. I know you need to chat with your other mate, but we can take it easy together. I don't think you should be alone until we get a solid plan laid out. We don't need you taking off on your own."

I roll my eyes. "You're right. It'll help me focus on something and not worry as much."

Chapter 14

After getting to my room, Vixie makes me plant myself on the couch and she fixes me a cup of tea.

"I know you're not much of a tea fan, but chamomile is relaxing and soothing." She hands me the steaming cup, and the smell does relax me.

"It smells pleasant. I'll let it cool off some before I sip on it. I need to chat with Zeke as it is. He's on his way to the vampire kingdom."

"Oh, it's so pretty there."

"So, I've been told. I hope to eventually get there to see it myself someday." I smile and then close my eyes, reaching through my bond to Zeke. I focus and put up a wall to make it where only we can communicate. That way our conversation doesn't bother Kai.

Hey, Zeke, my sisters were taken. I think it was Stole who took them.

Shit, so that's what I've been feeling with the bond. Are you okay?

My heart beats faster, thinking about what I want to do to their captor. *I'm as okay as I can be, considering the circumstances. Lucifer won't let me look for them, so Kai is sending out scouts. Lucifer wants me to wait until after my coming-out ball next week.*

I can send some out when I arrive at the palace. The quicker we get information, the better. I'm sure the vampires have been invited to attend, right?

According to Lucifer, they are. How far out are you from reaching them?

I have about thirty minutes on foot until I'm there.

Will you let me know what you find out about Ulric?

You know I will. Stop looking for things to worry about.

Ugh, you know I struggle with that.

I do but you can do this, Ember. We'll find them.

Thanks for the support, Zeke. Just hurry up and get here.

I'm working on it, love. I'll check in again soon.

I open my eyes and notice Vixie watching me curiously. "So, what did he say?"

"He's not happy about the situation either, but he'll know more once he makes it to the palace. Oh, he did say that he would send out some of the vampire scouts."

"That's good. With both parties sending out scouts, we'll find them in no time." Vixie plops down beside me.

"Yeah. What should we do in the meantime?" I ask, trying to ignore the stack of books on the table across the room.

"Don't you have a lot of reading to do? I mean, I know we both have some reading to do for Minerva, but you have way more than I do." Vixie shrugs.

"I was really hoping you wouldn't suggest that. I guess I should work on it though. Until I hear something from Zeke at least."

"Right. Now sip some tea and get to reading." Vixie nods at my cup.

I roll my eyes. "Yes, ma'am."

We sit together, sipping tea and reading for around an hour or two before Zeke's words fill my mind.

Ember, you aren't going to believe this, but Zuko brought Ulric here.

I sit upright, causing Vixie to shift and drop her book. She reaches down to pick it up as she looks at me curiously.

Is he okay? I send back, holding up my hand, letting Vixie know that I'll fill her in on the conversation in a moment.

Yes and no. His wounds are healed thanks to vampire blood, but he's in some weird coma. No one's been able to wake him from it. Zendaya has been traveling back and forth, keeping my father and Zuko up to date on things going on with Greed. He's planning to make a move on Lucifer soon, regardless of how many hellhounds he has.

How does he plan to do that?

She didn't say how. She's still trying to figure it out. She's also been helping us try to break through whatever is keeping Ulric in a coma.

Is there a way to bring him here? Maybe Minerva can help us figure out how to break him from it.

We can. I'll get plans to travel squared away with my father and my brother. We'll set out soon and bring extra stuff for your coming-out ball. My father is excited to meet you.

I blush and Vixie eyes me curiously. *I guess I'm excited to meet him too. I'm honestly nervous now.*

Don't be. You'll love him. I'll check in soon and let you know when we leave. It may be tomorrow. The scouts are going out this evening.

Great. We'll chat soon. I smile and turn my attention to Vixie. "Ulric is with the vampires. He's in some weird coma that they can't break. The Vamps are going to bring him to the estate with them. Zeke says the scouts are going out tonight and that he, Ulric, and the rest of his vampire party should be on their way here tomorrow."

She smiles. "That's good."

"Yes, I'm relieved, somewhat. He also mentioned that Greed may move ahead early in his plans to attack Lucifer somehow. Zendaya has been feeding them the info, but she's only getting bits and pieces. I think they're concerned about her trust now."

"That's not good. They don't have any idea when or what methods they'll use?"

"No, not yet. I'm sure they'll figure it out though. If Zendaya is still feeding them the intel, it's all a matter of time, right?"

"I hope so. We'll have to let Lucifer know and up the security. Especially with your ball coming up." Vixie frowns.

"We'll be ready, Vixie. Don't worry. He won't be able to do anything," I offer with confidence.

"I'm sure you're right." She shrugs. "Did they say anything specific about the coma?"

I let out a sigh. "No. The whole situation has them confused. He healed up with their blood, but he didn't wake up."

"Odd. That almost always works. Do you think Minerva will know something?"

"That's what I'm hoping for. She's good with all things magical. I'm going to have her look him over. I'll be happy just having him close again."

Vixie nods. "I'm curious to see how Kai and Ulric will do with having to get along. They've never been good at that."

"That's what Zendaya said. They're going to have to figure it out. I mean, they're both tied to me now."

Vixie smiles. "Is Lucifer going to announce them all as your mates at the ball?"

I blink, processing her words. "I think so? We haven't talked about it much. I guess I need to ask about the process. Arminda will know too, won't she?"

Vixie shrugs. "She may be doing most of the planning. I don't see Lucifer letting himself get wrapped up in that. Do you want them announced as your mates?"

I nod. "Yes, I just, is it common to have more than one mate for someone like me?"

Vixie shrugs. "No idea. You're the first heir to survive this long."

I sigh. "Good point. What exactly is my title?"

Vixie looks at me skeptically, "How do you not know? You're too far out of the loop. You're the princess of Hell. The only princess of Hell."

"Nothing else though?"

"I mean, I guess you'll also be considered a princess to the vampires since Zeke is a prince. Their king defers to Lucifer on some things but mostly rules with his own methods."

I shrug. "I'm okay with that." I reposition myself on the couch when Zeke's words come through.

Slight change in plans, love. We're leaving to come your way in the next hour. We should be there tomorrow sometime. We're taking the dragons.

I blink, processing his words and Vixie tilts her head, looking at me curiously. I hold my hand up in a gesture to imply that I'll share in a minute. *Okay, what?*

Zeke's chuckle burns down the line. *We're riding dragons. You'll have to see them. I hope they won't scare you much. They are magnificent and fun to ride.*

Holy cow. Will Ulric be fine, moving from there via dragon? How is he even getting transported?

He is going to ride in a large container that resembles a bus. We use it in wars to transport the wounded with dragons. He will be comfortable in it. I think the quicker we get him there the better, honestly. Being with you will hopefully help with the coma.

I sure hope so. I'm ready to see him again.

"What's going on over there? So many emotions have flitted across your face in the last few minutes." Vixie breaks my concentration and I laugh.

"Sorry. Zeke says they'll be here sooner than planned. They're leaving now and will arrive tomorrow. I was asking about the dragons he mentioned."

Vixie lifts her brows in surprise. "I didn't know they still had them. I haven't seen dragons in ages. The vampires have always been the ones to communicate with them."

I nod. "You'll have to share more with me about the dragons or maybe point me to a book. I didn't know they were real!"

"I will. I guess we better work on our studies for real now since they're going to arrive earlier. It'll throw our day off again. Not that I'll complain too much but we do have a lot on our plates." Vixie reaches for one of the spell books and flips it open.

"Ugh, you're right. I have too much to read as it is. You think I can have food brought to us from the kitchen? That way we can keep plugging away?" I look over at the door.

"Go for it. You can just run down the hall and ask. I'll hang out here."

"Okay, I'll do just that and then we can study, study, study." I smile cheerily, thinking how all my mates will finally be with me soon.

Chapter 15

The vampires arrive riding dragons. Each of them varies in color and it's late in the day as they land. A group of similar-looking dragons carries a large structure that seems to be made of stone or some type of metal. They set it down gently before landing beside it.

A whistle fills the air and I smile as Zeke slides off the back of a purple dragon. He sprints toward me and swings me up into the air. I giggle as he spins me, and he sets me down with a heavy kiss to my lips.

"I missed you, love. I see you've been doing well," he whispers into my ear.

"Me too. Can I see Ulric now?" I try to peer around him at the large structure.

"Yes, but be prepared."

I pull on his arm and try to make my way toward the structure only to be stopped by Zuko grabbing me and pulling me into a hug.

"Hey, little sister. I missed you," Zuko says.

"I missed you too, Zuko. Sorry, I'm really excited to see Ulric." I step back out of our embrace.

"Did Zeke tell you of his status? My father wants to meet you. He's right behind me." He points over his shoulder, and I see a man with dark black hair, golden eyes, and a runner's build. He's moving toward us as if gliding on air.

"Oh, uhm yes, Zeke did mention it." I step back and watch as the man comes closer.

He smiles at me as he stretches his tall frame. I guess riding dragons will cause anyone to cramp up from sitting too long. "Hello, Ember, daughter. It's nice to finally meet you. Both of my sons have spoken highly of you. You're much younger than I expected. My name is Absalom."

I blush. "Thanks, I guess. I hope they've only told you good things. Thank you for coming and for tending to Ulric. I would like to see him now if you don't mind."

"That's understandable, child. You've been separated from him for a long time and I'm hoping that having you close will pull him out of whatever is causing him to stay in a coma. With his immortal strength and healing abilities, he shouldn't be in one, but Zuko mentioned a strange white light surrounding him before he crash landed to the ground with his wound." Absalom nods toward the carrier.

I blink as my mind goes back to the battle. "I think that was from me. I'm not sure what it did or if it's the cause, but I guess we'll find out."

"Interesting," Absalom says, scratching his chin.

"I'll take you to him, Ember," Zuko says.

I nod and then look over my shoulder to Kai. "Are you coming?"

Kai smiles and nods before striding to my side. He shakes Zeke's hand, and we make our way to the last car behind Zuko.

My nerves give me butterflies and I brace myself to discover him thin and deathly. I grab both Zeke's and Kai's hands as Zuko opens the door.

I see a couple of vampires walking around, wearing long robes. A heart monitor rests next to a large bed where someone rests beneath a bright red blanket. It fascinates me briefly that they would have regular medical equipment but as I've learned, this realm is full of surprises.

I step into the carrier with Kai and Zeke next to me. I feel my body shake as I near and I drop both of my mates' hands as I step forward next to the bed. I rest a hand on the sheet and stare down at Ulric as he breathes in and out steadily.

His body remains the same as it was the last time I saw him, but his hair is longer. He has a scruffy beard and looks as if he were sleeping.

Ulric, can you hear me? I stare at him, hoping to hear something. *Come back to me, love. I'm here. We're safe.*

I slide my hand up his arm and cup his face. His skin is warm, but he doesn't move. I frown and fight the tears that attempt to force their way out. I need to get him to Minerva.

"Can we move him inside? I'm going to have Minerva look him over," I ask one of the robed, male vampires.

"Yes, just show us where and we'll move the bed and set up everything," he says with a flourish of his hand.

"He'll need to be taken to my quarters. I'll lead the way," I say and grab both Kai and Zeke by the hand, pulling them out.

As we step on the ground, I hear something shift behind me and I turn to see a larger door open with a ramp that drops down. The medical vamps turn Ulric's bed and push it out. They nod to me, and we begin walking toward the estate.

As we walk, I have to remind myself where the elevator is. There is only one in the entire estate.

Sensing my thoughts, Kai squeezes my hand. "If we go this way, we can take the elevator up to our designated floor."

I smile at Kai and squeeze his hand in thanks as we adjust our direction to make our way to the elevator.

In no time at all, we reach our floor and make our way silently down the hall. I push open my door and find Arminda sitting at my table. She stands but pauses when she sees the vampires pushing a bed through the door.

It surprises me that it fits but I motion toward the sitting area. Arminda catching on to what we're doing begins moving furniture around.

Once we get the bed situated and the vampires have his medical equipment set up, I ask Arminda to retrieve Minerva.

I move to sit on the edge of Ulric's bed while we wait. Kai and Zeke lounge on the couch. The medical vampires check Ulric's vitals and then leave us to relax in peace until Minerva arrives.

"Do you think Minerva will know what to do?" Zeke asks curiously.

I glance down at Ulric. "I hope so. I don't know who else would. She helped figure out the time issue. If she doesn't know right away, maybe she has a book that'll help?"

Kai's deep voice soothes the knot trying to form in my throat. "She'll know what to do. She's been around for a long time."

We sit, peacefully waiting until Arminda and Minerva walk through the door. I watch them move closer and observe the stern expression on Minerva's face.

"How long has he been like this?" she asks us and I turn to Zeke.

Zeke stands and moves closer. "A couple of months."

Minerva nods and holds both of her hands up over his body. A golden light glows from her palms as she moves them in a clockwise circle over his body. She does this for a good five minutes before dropping her hands.

She turns to me. "I think I know what we can do. I'll need to grab a black candle and we need a knife."

"I think I have those. Let me check." I quickly move to the cabinets and find a small black tealight candle. I walk back to Minerva and pull out one of my daggers from one of the many hidden pockets I have on my pants.

She takes them from my hand and then flicks her wrist at the small fireplace across the room. A fire ignites and warms the room around us.

"Ember, I need you to take the knife and cut a slit in both yours and Ulric's right palms. You will then let your blood mingle while I light this candle and perform the spell. After the spell ends, it will pull energy from you and bring Ulric out of his coma. He may struggle to come up so make sure you start speaking to him when you feel him begin to surface." Minerva places the small candle on the end of the bed between his feet.

"Will my bond strengthen when he surfaces? How will I know?" I ask.

Minerva chuckles. "You'll feel it, my dear. Now, let's get started. Everyone else, step back. If this first attempt doesn't work, I have another approach."

I nod and hold my dagger steadily in my hand. With a deep breath, I slice my hand, letting my breath out as my skin parts. I stare at the cut as it starts to bleed momentarily before I reach down to grab Ulric's hand. I slice his hand easily and line our cuts up. Pressing our palms together, I feel the warm liquid smear between us as Minerva begins to chant softly.

I can't make out her words as she chants but I can smell that the candle is lit. I watch and listen internally for something along the bond. A light stinging sensation spirals through my hand where I hold on to Ulric, but I fight against the reaction to pull it away. Instead, I start speaking to Ulric down our line.

Ulric, can you hear me? I need you to fight your way up. I'm sorry you're in this weird coma. I think it's my fault, but I don't really know. Please come back to me.

The stinging turns into a burning pain, and I cringe. It feels like I'm resting my hand in a fire.

Ulric, please. I'm begging you. Come back. I love you. I need you. I feel tears escape and slide down my cheeks as I continue to hold his hand.

The pain continues to burn, and it's all the way up my arm. My energy is seeping into him now.

Ember? His voice is tentative, questioning whether it's really me.

Yes, Ulric! Come back.

I'm trying but I'm weak. I can feel your energy pouring in, but I don't think it's enough.

I continue holding his hand and turn to Minerva over my shoulder. "I can hear him and converse with him, but he says there isn't enough energy. What do we do?"

Minerva frowns. "I was afraid of that. Kai, go fetch Vixie and quickly. If Ember doesn't have enough energy, Vixie's magic will be the only other strong enough."

Kai nods. "I'll be back quickly."

Zeke, sounding supportive, says, "Just hang in there, Ember. You too, Ulric, if you can hear me."

I can hear them, Ember. Why is Kai hanging around?

I roll my eyes as I turn back to look at Ulric's still form. *Of all the things to ask right now, that's the one thing that stands out?*

I mean, yeah, it does, but then again, I know I've missed a lot. Why is he getting Zendaya's daughter?

Well, Vixie and I can perform spells. We're working on building up to wordless ones but apparently our magic is strong. We reversed the spell that caused an imbalance between the realms regarding time. Everything is now in sync.

Okay, but that doesn't explain Kai. Are we at Lucifer's? He found you?

Right, forget you missed that too. I let out a long sigh and start from the last time we saw each other. It helps fill the time as I explain it to him. As Kai returns with Vixie, Ulric stops mid-story.

So, you're saying Kai is your mate too? What the hell? How many men do I have to share you with? I don't know how I feel about this.

Well, that's too bad. You're stuck with it. You'll learn to get along with him. Can we talk more about this after I get you awake? Vixie is here and I need her help.

Fine.

I glance over at Vixie who is speaking with Minerva. I think she's explaining what needs to be done. At least, I hope she is.

"Thanks for coming, Vixie." I smile at her as she moves to Ulric's other side.

"Any time. Plus, he's family, right? I'm doing this for you though, Ember. Hand me that dagger." She reaches over Ulric, and I place my dagger in her open palm, handle first.

She pulls it from my grasp and slices her palm open, letting blood pool up before she slices Ulric's.

Motherfucker, what was that? What are you women doing to me? I almost laugh at his words but the burning in my arm intensifies and Vixie gasps.

"Hang in there, Vixie, the pain gets worse. Hopefully we can do this quickly." She nods at my words, and we focus on Ulric's supine form.

Ulric, try now, I coax after a few minutes.

Here goes nothing. I feel my bond growing stronger and I notice his eyes fluttering.

Keep going. You can do it. I love you, I encourage him.

Ulric's eyes continue to flutter and finally, after two minutes, he opens them and gasps loudly. A pulse of energy bursts from the three of us, displacing the furniture around us and he sits up.

Vixie and I drop his hands and I throw myself at him. He catches me but falls back into the bed. Tears stream down my face as he hugs me tightly.

"You brought me out of it, little wolf." He nuzzles into my hair.

"I've missed you so much. Please don't ever do that again." I cry and bury my head in his chest.

His low chuckle vibrates through my ears. "I don't plan on it. I felt like I was trapped in ice. It was strange. I didn't hurt but I couldn't get out either. Can we sit up again?"

I sniff and pull back. "Sorry. I couldn't help myself."

Ulric sits up and looks around the room. He takes a moment to take in the disheveled furniture and the people gathered around him.

"So, we're at Lucifer's estate? When did it get to be so nice? Why does he have electricity? Who are all the extra people here?" He looks around and scratches his head.

I smile as I pull his hand down. "Slow down. Let's do all this one step at a time. The other's you don't recognize are Minerva, my witch teacher, and Arminda, my tutor. You know Kai and Vixie. Zeke you knew was here by his voice. The robed vampires have been caring for you. Sorry, I don't know their names."

Ulric nods. Then he growls, looking at Kai. "How did you mate to my mate too?"

Kai lifts his hands in a peaceful gesture. "Calm down. Fate decides that. I couldn't control it. Did you react like this with Zeke?"

Zeke snorts. "He kind of did. We worked through it. We'll figure this all out as we go. Now that you're awake, Ulric, I think we need to fill you in on things and be alone with our mate."

I hum in approval before clearing my throat. "I like that idea." I turn to Minerva. "Thank you for helping me."

"It was my pleasure, dear. I think you and Vixie are ready to learn some harder stuff now so plan on a change in your learning, starting tomorrow. Finish those books I have you working on tonight though. I leave you to reunite with your mates." Minerva smiles, bowing lightly, before turning to leave.

I turn to look at Vixie. "I couldn't have done that without your help. We make an awesome pair. Care to join us at dinner tonight with Lucifer?"

She shakes her head. "I love that I could help but I'm going to take a hard pass on dining with the king of Hell tonight. I need to rest after that. I'll see you in the morning."

I move around the bed to wrap her in a hug before she goes. I see the vampire medics slip out with her and I turn my attention to Arminda.

"I'm assuming you would like to pass on our studies today. Very well, that's fine. I'll let your father know you'll have all your mates tonight at dinner. He may come around beforehand. He had planned to be there when Zeke arrived with the other vampires but apparently there is some type of skirmish happening in a town near the portal to Heaven. He's been speaking with Cerberus on it," Arminda voices.

"My uncle is here?" Kai asks, looking at her.

"He is. I believe he may stay for dinner. I'm not sure. I'll tell him to give you all some peace for the afternoon though. I'll see you tomorrow, Ember." Arminda smiles before turning toward the door.

"Thanks, Arminda!" I say to her retreating figure. She waves a hand over her shoulder before she steps into the hall.

"Can someone finish filling me in on the things I missed?" Ulric looks between us all and I laugh.

"We will, but first, do you want something to eat? Dinner is still a few hours off and I'm starving after expending that much energy." I move toward the cabinet and find some bread and peanut butter. "Peanut butter sandwiches anyone?"

"I'll take one, I guess. I've never had one before," Ulric states, looking at me curiously.

"You will love it," I say and hear Zeke and Kai chuckle. I fix the sandwiches for everyone, and we sit down on the couches after we put them up right. "Do you want me to start where I left off earlier?"

Ulric bites into his sandwich and smiles. "Yes, that is a great place to start. Also, this is really good."

"I knew you would like it. Okay, I'll start after I met Kai." This causes Ulric to grunt but I launch into the story.

I fill him in on everything that's happened since I escaped his father. I leave nothing out and even share with him the bits and pieces of what's been going on in the pack. At the end, he's rubbing his head as if a headache is setting in.

"I'm sorry, does your head hurt now? I can get you something."

"I think I'll be okay. How much longer do we have until dinner?" Ulric asks, looking around.

"I think about an hour." Kai shrugs.

"I think I want to nap until then. Ember, will you stay with me?" Ulric grabs my hand.

I nod. "Of course."

"I'll give you guys some space for a bit. I need to go check in on my father and brother. I'll be back before we have to go to dinner though," Zeke says and moves forward, placing a kiss on my lips.

"Okay, I'll see you in a bit." I smile as he breezes away.

Kai clears his throat. "I'm going to check and see if we've heard anything from the scouts. I'll be back around the same time Zeke gets here. Ulric, rest up." Kai moves forward and pulls me into his arms. He places a lingering kiss on my lips. "I love you. See you in a bit."

"I love you, too," I say, squeezing Kai once more. I watch as he moves into the hall before turning back to Ulric. "How about we move to my bed and get you out of that awkward hospital bed? I think it'll be more comfortable for you."

Ulric nods and moves to stand. He rests his feet on the ground but when he pushes up, his knees buckle. I catch him and have him gently lean on my shoulder as he regains his balance.

"Let's take it easy. Your legs aren't used to the weight anymore even though the muscle is still there."

Ulric grunts. "I'll get it soon. I think I just need a bit more rest."

"I'll help you get there," I say and push open my bedroom door. We make our way slowly as we walk the remainder of the distance to the bed.

Once we're at the bed, Ulric is able to climb in and slide under the blankets easily. He lets out a loud sigh as he lies back on the pillows. "This is nicer than my bed back at home. Having the luxury of electricity is wonderful. I don't know why my father won't embrace it."

I shrug. "Beats me, but let's not talk about him. You need to rest."

"You're right, little wolf. Come here and let me hold you. I've missed you." He reaches for me and pulls me into his side.

"I've missed you too. I thought you were dead, Ulric. Let's not ever do that again." I snuggle in closer.

He grunts and tightens his hold around me. I listen to his breaths as they even out. Soon, he falls asleep. I double-check that he's still okay before letting myself drift off with him. The spell to wake him really did take it out of me. Will I ever be able to perform the difficult ones without so much fatigue?

Chapter 16

Kai wakes me later and I see Zeke leaning against the bedroom wall behind him. I stretch and nudge Ulric who thankfully wakes as well. I climb from the bed and get scooped up by Kai who pulls me in for a kiss.

"The scouts picked up a trail that they think belongs to your sisters. It's quite a way out though and too close to the gate to Heaven for my comfort. They're going to do so more hunting to confirm it. It's where the skirmishes are. I stopped by and spoke with my uncle, and he said he would send out a group as well." Kai sets me on my feet, and I wrap my arms around him.

"That's great news. If he can confirm it, maybe I can talk Lucifer into postponing the ball." I move around Kai toward my closet. Zeke pushes off the wall and moves toward me while I hear Ulric climb from the bed. Thankfully, his knees don't buckle this time.

Ulric's gruff voice is deep as he asks, "Is it possible to get a change of clothes?"

Zeke pauses with me by the wardrobe and kisses me on the cheek. He then turns toward Ulric. "Arminda brought some stuff in for you while you were sleeping. It's lying on the couch."

"Excellent, how soon do we need to leave?" Ulric asks, moving toward the living room.

Kai says, "About ten minutes, maybe less. We let you both rest as much as possible. How are you feeling, Ulric?"

Ulric grunts as he passes through the door, then calls over his shoulder, "Much better than before. Thanks for asking."

Kai grunts in response and I can't help but wonder if this is how the two of them will communicate going forward. At least they aren't trying to kill each other.

"Any other news?" I ask, looking at Kai and moving toward him. He wraps me in his arms, and I snuggle in close.

"None that I know of. You feel, okay?" He kisses the top of my head.

"Yeah, just a little groggy still. I'm just happy to have the three of you here with me."

Zeke comes up behind me and rests his chin on my shoulder. "Us too. We do have a lot of adjusting to do though as a couple. I mean, three males and one female. Things might be a bit stiff at times."

I glare at him. "Did you just make a sexual joke or were you talking about how we'll have to get used to working in sync."

Zeke shrugs while Kai chuckles. "Take it as you will, love. Are you worried?"

I cast a look over at Kai and then toward the living room. "A little."

Kai sighs. "I promise not to aggravate him, or start a fight, if it will bother you. I'm sure Ulric will be on his best behavior as well."

Ulric walks back in, pulling on a clean shirt. "What am doing? I heard something about being on my best behavior. When am I not?"

I snort. "I can think of a few occasions."

Ulric points a finger at me. "You're hard to resist so those times don't count."

I roll my eyes. "Anyway. I know you and Kai have had beef with each other in the past. I want you two to be able to get along. Can you both do that or at least try?"

Ulric eyes Kai and Kia lifts his brow. The two stare at each other for several minutes before Ulric concedes, "I think we can manage. Are you ready to go, Ember?"

I glance down at the clothes I slid into from the wardrobe. It's nothing fancy but I've never felt pressure to dress up for dinner with Lucifer. He has yet to comment about what I wear. "Yep. Let's go. It's just down the hall."

Zeke leads us into the living area and moves to open the door for us all. I smile at him as I lead us through the entry, and he pinches me. *You look good, love. I think you and I need some alone time later.*

I smirk over my shoulder as I move down the hall. *That can be arranged, although I'm curious to see how having all three of you will work. Can we try that?*

Zeke chuckles behind me as he closes the door. *I'm sure we can. Whatever you wish.*

Kai rushes past me to get the door to the dining hall and I smile as he opens it for me. Entering the room, I notice a tall muscular man sitting next to Lucifer. He has auburn hair and a short scruffy beard. His eyes are silver, and he smiles at us.

"Ah, Ember. I see you have all your mates with you finally. Ulric, it's a pleasure to see you healthy. I take it whatever Ember did, worked?" Lucifer smiles merrily, taking us all in.

Kai passes me to sit next to the man with Lucifer and motions for me to sit next to him. I nod and follow as Ulric responds to Lucifer.

"It did although she did have some help. The three ladies broke me out of whatever had me under." He smiles and takes the chair next to Zeke.

The auburn-haired man smiles and says with a deep voice, "I'm Cerberus. Ember, it's a pleasure to meet you. I've met your mates all at some point in the past and of course you know Kai is my nephew. You have a strong group with these three."

"It's nice to meet you too. Lucifer, do you know what may have caused Ulric's coma? Minerva didn't mention anything. All I remember is a bright white light shooting from me and encircling him before I was taken through the gate."

Lucifer frowns. "That, my dear, may have been a protective healing spell gone awry. That's what it sounds like. I've only known of that happening one other time in my life and the mate had to be the main one to bring the other back. It always requires a lot of energy, and it almost killed the being."

Zeke asks my thought before I can. "Who was it?"

Lucifer takes a sip of wine from the glass resting before him. "It was Wrath. His mate brought him back. It almost killed her to do it."

I tilt my head to the side as the butlers bring in wine and plates of food for us. "How did she manage not to let it consume her? I couldn't even handle it alone."

Lucifer swirls his glass and I notice Cerberus stiffen.

"His mate was an angel at the time. Her name was Noel. The two fell in love at the beginning of time before our fall and she left Heaven to save him. He and I had a heated fight that turned deadly. I still regret that fight at times, but since she saved him and gave up her place through the gate, we've been on better terms."

I pick up my own glass and take a sip before speaking. "Wow. That is beautiful but sad."

Cerberus speaks up. "It was. Lucifer was inconsolable at the time. For the record though, Wrath did take out the woman he loved during that time. I don't remember the reasoning Wrath had. I do remember it was stupid. Lucifer doesn't love very often, and that was one of the times he did. It was a big ordeal."

Lucifer glowers at Cerberus. "I wasn't going to share that."

I look at Lucifer curiously. "Was she your mate?"

He shakes his head. "No. I haven't found that individual yet. Although," he points his glass at Kai, "I have renewed hope thanks to you two."

Ulric adds, "It could happen. It's always when you least expect it."

"You can say that again," Zeke says with a chuckle. "Or you could have them stare you in the face for years and deny it."

"Is that what you did with Ember?" Kai asks curiously.

Zeke nods. "I was drawn to her from the day she was born. It freaked me out because she was a baby at the time. I had these overprotective instincts, and I assumed it was because I was friends with Kyra. Once her power started to awaken, I was blown away. I couldn't deny it anymore, but she was tied up with the wolves Corey and Adam."

I blush at Zeke's confession. Then add, "You could have said something earlier on."

Zeke snorts. "Right. Because that would have gone over well. You had enough trouble hiding your relationship with Corey from the pack as it was."

"I managed though, didn't I?" I shrug.

Lucifer laughs. "You are quite the troublemaker aren't you, daughter?"

Kai laughs as well. "That she is. Have I shared her story of what she did to Charity?"

Lucifer looks proud. "I know it, but I think you should share it with the rest of our party. They would enjoy it, I believe."

I groan. "Do we have to? I mean, I thought she was sleeping with him still, so I had a reason to intervene, right?"

Kai throws me a look and I roll my eyes as he dives into the story of that day I beat the shit out of Charity. Of course, the rest of the guys, including Cerberus, laugh their heads off. I can't help but smile. Lucifer sits, sipping his wine with a proud look. I guess that's good, right?

"She really can kick some ass when it comes to the ones she loves. It's one of the things I love about her." Ulric beams at me from where he sits next to Zeke.

"Let's just hope my beast mode is enough for us to win against Greed when that all goes down?" I reach for one of the bottles of wine in the middle of the table. We've all been done eating for a while now, but the conversation keeps flowing.

"What do you mean a battle with Greed? I haven't heard anything about it," Cerberus chimes in and looks at Lucifer expectantly.

Lucifer lets out a loud sigh. "Greed has been kidnapping shifters to build a hellhound army to take me on. He had Ember for a time but somehow, she managed to stay under the radar and kept her identity a secret."

"She had help with that," Ulric adds proudly.

Lucifer nods. "I am thankful for that. Greed has apparently been planning this for some time, but Ember threw a wrench in his plans. The spies I sent haven't gotten much, but Prince Zuko and King Absalom reported intel they received from Zendaya. She's keeping tallies on things. She helped Ember as well."

Cerberus frowns. "Are they behind the fights breaking out near the gate? It's been peaceful there for years and then out of the blue, these guys show up and things start happening."

Lucifer shrugs. "We'll find out in time. Have you not found anything on them?"

Cerberus shakes his head. "They've been pretty evasive."

"Well, if what's going on is related to Greed and whatever is going on there, our scouts should show up there. We think Greed may be behind the recent disappearance of Ember's younger sisters. Maybe they are there?" Kai suggests.

I stiffen and look at Lucifer. He meets my gaze with concern in his eyes. I turn back to Kai. "Didn't you say the lead they found was too close to the gate to Heaven for comfort?"

He nods. "I did."

Zeke adds, "Could everything be coming to a head and your sisters are there?"

Ulric grunts and then Cerberus speaks up, "I'll send more of my troops out. We'll have something for you hopefully before your ball next week."

"I would rather go and look myself." I growl.

Lucifer growls in return. "It's not happening. You are too important to put your life at risk."

Anger rises and I feel my power surge as my wings flare. "I would give my life for those girls. They are my sisters. What's keeping me from going?"

Lucifer's eyes glow red and his wings flare as mine did.

Tension fills the room at the display of power. "You will not go. I will not lose another child because you won't let our warriors do their jobs."

Kai moves his hand to my leg. "We won't let her go, Lucifer. You can trust us as her mates that she'll remain safe. We're going to pour all our resources into finding them, Ember, don't worry."

I settle back and let my wings relax as I continue to stare at Lucifer. He relaxes as well but his eyes still glow. I wonder if mine do as well.

Cerberus breaks the tension. "Well, you definitely have his temper, that's for sure. I thought you seemed too docile earlier but there it is."

I turn my gaze to him, and he chuckles.

"I'll have more of my team move on it as soon as I return tomorrow. We'll help you find them."

I smile. "Thank you. I appreciate that. After the ball, if you haven't found anything, we'll join you. Lucifer said I could do that at least." I glance over at Lucifer as he rolls his eyes.

"You're so stubborn."

I wink at him. "Apparently, I have a double dose of it."

Chapter 17

After dinner, the guys and I make our way back to my room. I'm thankful that the four-poster bed is large, and that there is enough room for all of us in it. "How do you guys want to do this?" I pause at the end of the bed and turn to face them.

They glance at each other and then turn their gazes to me. A mischievous look dances in their eyes and Zeke steps forward and wraps me in his arms. "There are many ways we can do this, love. I thought you knew that. I'll take the lead on this one." He leans in and kisses my neck.

"What do you mean, oh." I'm caught off guard as he spins me, and we land at the edge of the bed. He slides his hand up my shirt and my mind stutters. I can suddenly feel the emotions of all my mates and how aroused they are watching Zeke with me.

Holy shit, I send out and they chuckle.

I feel another set of hands on my shoulders, and I pull back enough to see Ulric behind me. Kai kneels on the bed beside him and reaches for my waist. I'm pulled back and my top is removed at the same time.

I blink as my mates surround me, all eyeing me with glowing eyes. I glance down to see how aroused they are and smile wickedly. This should be fun.

I lean back and grab Ulric around the neck, encouraging him to lean forward to kiss me. His lips seal over mine and I feel Kai snake his hands around to my breasts. Zeke busies himself removing my shoes and then my pants. I feel them slide gently down my legs moments later and a trail of heated kisses begins at the base of my ankle, slowly moving up.

I anticipate Zeke's motions, but Kai slides his hand gently down before Zeke makes it all the way up and begins to tease me. He circles my clit with his callused hands, sending spikes of pleasure coursing through my body.

I moan into Ulric's lips, and I feel his hand begin to explore my chest. My nipples are hard beneath his touch, and I gasp as Zeke's lips meet my sex.

I moan loudly as Zeke's tongue tastes me and slides in and out. Ulric moves down and takes my nipple in his mouth and Kai moves up to kiss me. I'm lost in pleasure as I reach my first climax. It makes me feel high and I crave more.

I sense my mates rotating around me and I glance down to see Ulric lining himself up with me. His clothes are gone, and I take a moment to look around at Zeke and Kai. They remain clothed.

Ulric slides in and moans as he pushes deeper. I clench around him, taking him in. It's been so long since he and I had sex. I forgot how large he is. He pumps in and out gently as my other two mates begin to play with my breasts again.

Ulric grips my waist as his movements become harder and he pushes deeper. I moan loudly as he speeds up and I feel myself climbing again. The sensation is fucking glorious, and I can't get enough.

Harder and faster, he moves in me until I feel myself plummeting off the edge. I scream out and feel him follow me into orgasmic bliss. I feel him slide out of me and gently rest his head on my stomach.

I look down into his eyes. "Wow," is all I get out.

"Shower time," Kai says in my ear, and I turn to him. He has an eager smile on his face, and I can only guess what's coming next.

Zeke and Kai help me off the bed as Ulric removes himself from between my legs. They lead me to the shower, shedding clothes as they move, and my heart skips a beat. They are going to wear me out tonight.

Zeke turns on the water and tests it while Kai slides his hands up and down my waist. The movement is calming but also arousing. Heck, being around them while they're naked is arousing in and of itself. Will I ever tire of seeing them like this?

Kai slaps me on the butt, bringing me back to focus and I step into the steaming water of the shower. It feels magnificent as it pours down my body, washing the sweat away. I hear the guys step in behind me and I turn to find all three of them standing with me in the shower. Once again, I'm thankful for the luxury of my rooms and that there is a giant-ass shower. With all three of them in here with me, it feels small.

Looking at Kai, I see the eagerness in his expression again as he steps forward. I watch him closely as I try to figure out what he's planning. He pulls me to him, but instead of standing with my legs wrapped around him, he pushes me to the wall to slide home. He seats himself deep and begins to pump in and out. I scream out his name as he bites into my shoulder and faintly growls.

I open my eyes and see Ulric and Zeke watching us hungrily, but pleasure takes control of my brain again as Kai reaches down with one hand to pinch my clit. I come again and feel him follow behind me. He catches me as my legs become jelly and I feel another set of hands grab me.

Opening my eyes, I see Zeke pulling me from Kai's hold. "Now we clean you. I'll have my turn with you soon. I'm not missing out."

"Mm, you're all going to kill me. Then again, death by sex isn't a bad way to go," I murmur.

Zeke chuckles and continues to hold me close as he washes my body. He takes his time, scrubbing me down with the scented soaps. I feel pampered. As he starts to wash around my breasts, my nipples stand at attention once again and my sex clenches.

"Zeke, I want you now," I say as he continues to circle my nipples with soapy hands.

"Do you, love? Shall I make you wait?" Zeke purrs.

I whimper and he laughs. He spins me around and lifts me, gently placing both of my legs around his waist. It's a show of strength as he gently slides his shaft into me and holds me steady. He doesn't push me into the wall like Kai did minutes earlier but holds me beneath the steady stream of water.

Sensations pour down on me, overwhelming my senses as he pushes in and out at a gentle pace. It's like he's caressing me from the inside out. Where the other two were harder and faster, he's taking his time. It's a huge change and I love it. Each of my mates has their own way of showing me exactly how much they care.

"Oh, Zeke, don't stop," I say and he changes his tempo. I feel myself spiraling once again and he and I explode together. I swear the air around us feels warmer as he lowers us to the floor of the shower.

I rest my head against his as he murmurs, "I love you, Ember."

"I love you, Zeke. I love all three of you." I lift my head and see that Ulric and Kai are no longer in the shower. "Hey, where did they go?"

Zeke chuckles as he slides from my body. "They left shortly after I took you into my arms. I think we've all worn ourselves out."

We remain seated on the floor of the shower. "You can say that again. I'm officially worn out myself."

He brushes my wet hair behind my ear. "That you are. Let's get out and dry off, then we too can get some rest."

We stand from the floor, and he flips the water off. Thankfully, the heat lingers but the cool air from outside the shower rushes in and cools me as soon as the door opens. I quickly grab one of the towels resting on the vanity that I'm sure either Kai or Ulric placed there and wrap up in it.

Zeke chuckles as he steps out, steam rising from his body. "You look cold, love."

"I am," I respond, moving from the bathroom to my room in search of clothes. I'm stopped in my tracks though by the two bodies sprawled across my bed, snoring. "I guess they really were tired, huh?"

Zeke moves up behind me, wrapping me in his arms, his towel around his waist. "Well, making love to you does a number on us."

"Mhm, well, maybe it'll put Kai in a good mood, and he won't try to kill us all at training in the morning."

Zeke snorts. "I highly doubt that. Go get some clothes or don't. I don't think any of us will mind if you snuggle up to us naked."

"I think you would all very much enjoy that. Let's get some sleep. Tomorrow is going to be a very busy day." I push out of Zeke's hold and grab his hand, pulling him toward the bed.

"Nuh-uh, I'm putting boxers on at least. I'm not comfortable sleeping in a bed nude with those two just yet. You can stay naked though," Zeke exclaims, moving toward the living area.

"Oh fine. I'll save you a spot." I roll my eyes as he disappears into the other room and climb over my other mates who are sprawled at the end of the bed. They each have sweatpants on and look comfortable, so I crawl beneath my comforter and wait for Zeke. He joins me minutes later and snuggles up with me. I fall effortlessly into slumber with him wrapped around me.

Chapter 18

Kai gets us all up way too early and drags us out to the training field. I left a note for Arminda just in case she comes for our morning review. I don't think she'll be too upset that I left to train early. Then again, she may be. I am so behind on reading the material for her and Minerva. Although, she did say she might postpone.

I feel sore in places I forgot existed after our long night of lovemaking but strangely rejuvenated. Having all my mates with me fills me with renewed strength. I feel like we're unstoppable.

As we approach the training area, I see Vixie sprawled out, stretching. She's early too. She waves at us all and I head toward her. Kai stops the guys and I hear him ask them to assist him with setting up some things for us to practice with today.

"So, how was your night?" Vixie asks, lifting her brows suggestively.

I blush. "Busy."

She snorts. "I bet it was. What was it like having three guys?"

My blush turns crimson, and my face feels warm. "Do we really have to talk about this right now?"

"Fine. Next time we're alone, I want details. I can't help but be curious."

I roll my eyes. "Okay, but maybe we need to get you laid. I sense it's been a while."

She playfully slaps my arm. "It has but I'll be fine. I know where to go when I need something. Oh, look, here come Blaze and Leon. They look confused."

I turn and watch as our other teammates approach. Their attention seems to be on Kai, Zeke, and Ulric across the field. I notice them setting up large poles and that worries me. What is Kai planning for us to do to-day?

"Hey, guys, how's it going?" I ask loudly to Blaze and Leon, and they turn their attention to us as they close the distance between us.

"Morning. We're good. Who are our new friends?" Leon drops down next to me.

"They look strong." Blaze sits next to Vixie.

"They're Ember's other mates. I could have sworn you've met them both before. Prince Ezekiel of the vampires and Greed's son Prince Ulric." Vixie smiles and I blush once again.

"Damn, girl. You're bringing in the royalty. Wow," Leon says.

Blaze glances over at them. "I guess they look somewhat familiar. Are they training with us this morning?"

I nod. "Yes. We all need to be in tip-top shape. We may be leaving on a mission soon."

"Yes, finally! I feel like our last one was ages ago." Blaze cheers.

"That's because the last one you two went on was. You ended up drunk in a bar and almost got your dicks chopped off by the person we were after, remember?" Vixie places her hands on her hips sassily.

Leon shakes his head. "That's what we get for letting her fix our drinks. I swear she put something in them. We only had two!"

"Yeah, you keep telling yourself that, Leon. There were glasses ev-erywhere when we got there." Vixie quirks her brow.

"Only because you had just missed an intense bar fight between two lesser demons. It was over spilled beer. So stupid," Blaze says as he begins to stretch.

"Okay that's a crazy story. You're going to have to tell me more of the details sometime. On a different note, what are they setting up?" I point to where my mates are creating some strange obstacle course. There is a line of tall wooden poles leading up to a massive tangle of ropes that hang from hoops.

"Oh, fuck, not that again. He's setting up what has been termed the spider's web. We fought these strange spider-like demons years ago that lived in a cave filled with webs. We almost didn't make it out because we got lost in them and our senses were thrown off. He's simulating that for us, from what it looks like." Leon groans.

"Grrreeaattt," I drag out, staring at them as they finish setting up the last of the course. "We're going to get our asses handed to us once again?"

"Probably, just make sure you don't set it on fire. I did that and had to do extra conditioning on top of trying to create a new set of ropes. It's fucking confusing to build. I don't know how Kai makes them." Blaze scratches his head as he squints.

"I'm not sure he actually builds them. I think he purchases them from someone," Vixie adds.

"Okay, so no flames. Got it. Is it timed?" I look at my teammates and they all nod. "Fun," I say sarcastically.

We continue to stretch in silence, and I watch as my mates play around on the course they created to make sure things will stay in place. Zeke manages to make it through the ropes surprisingly fast and I stare opened mouth as he goes through again and tightens ropes. Once they've deemed it complete with head nods to each other, they make their way toward the four of us as we continue to stretch.

"Good morning, everyone. I want to introduce Zeke and Ulric. They'll be helping us this morning. Once you have all passed the obstacle course in ten minutes or less, you'll each rotate with us, working with various weapons," Kai announces in his deep voice, looking at Vixie, Blaze, Leon, and me.

"How many attempts do we get on this one?" Blaze asks and I nod, hoping for several attempts.

Kai smiles eagerly. "You each only get two. Ten minutes is more than enough time for you to make it through the course. The only challenging section is the spider ropes."

"Easy for you to say," I grumble and Kai shoots me a look. I roll my eyes in response.

"Pay attention to where you place your feet and grip, and you'll make it through just fine," Zeke says trying to be supportive. Ulric grunts.

"Vixie, you're up first," Kai says and points to the course. "Oh, and no magic allowed. I don't know if you and Ember know anything that might help you get through the course or not but I'm placing that rule down. Physical abilities only today."

Vixie mock salutes him. "Yes, sir!"

Kai growls and Vixie laughs as she moves toward the start of the course where a simple wall is set up. It must be scaled to reach the start of the next section where we must jump from pole to pole until we reach the spider's web.

Vixie scans the wall before placing her hands on it. I squint as I notice her slide her fingers into a small crack before placing the edge of her toe in another. She does this and climbs the wall easily but slowly. It's fascinating that she chose to do that. I would have never thought to use the small crevices in such a way. Then again, I've never had to scale a wall.

She moves on to the poles and I watch as she moves with a dancer's grace across them. She easily keeps her balance as the poles wobble slightly beneath her weight. She moves quick, dashing from one to the other, until she reaches the small platform at the start of the spider's web.

I see her pause and take a deep breath, before stepping into the mess of ropes. It's impossible to see her through the tangles but I can see the ropes dip at times. I thought it would be a straight through path, but it doesn't appear like it from the way the ropes bulge at times. Vixie spends longer in the web but finally, as the timer nears the ten-minute mark, she pops out at the other end and dashes to the flag marking the end of the course.

She doubles over by the flag, and I can tell she's breathing heavy. Neither of us rested after performing that spell yesterday to break Ulric from his coma. I know I'll be just as tired as she is once I make it through the course.

"Okay, Leon, you're up next. Ember will go last," Kai says and I frown.

Why are you making me go last? I send to Kai.

He doesn't make eye contact with me but instead watches Leon. *It'll be more of a challenge. I have to push you harder so you'll be ready for what may come. You'll have to face harder foes than any of your teammates and you know it. Being the heir, you have to be one of the best.*

I huff and glare at him. *That is stupid.*

It is what it is, Ember. Your safety matters more to me than your fatigue. You can do it. Kai sounds supportive, and I let my shoulders sag.

I watch as Leon makes it through, barely making the time, followed by Blaze. Both struggled with the web just as Vixie did and almost failed.

Taking a deep breath, I begin my trek to the start of the obstacle course and hit the ground running as soon as I hear the timer start. I follow Vixie's example and use the cracks to scale the wall. It's more difficult that I thought it would be, but I manage and make it to the top.

I stare down at the poles, forming a path that will be the best one to take to get me to the web. Once decided, I jump nimbly from pole to pole, barely staying on one for more than a second as I utilize my enhanced speed.

In no time, I'm standing before the web and the first thing I notice is that it's pitch black. No light comes from within the webs, and it astounds me. How is that even possible? Pushing my senses to the limits, I enter the ropes. I immediately feel lost, and I have yet to move from the entry. The light from where I was previously standing is gone. It's as if the obstacle swallowed me whole.

I tentatively move forward and let my nose take in the scents around me. I notice a heavy smell of dust and dirt lingering in the air. It's over-whelming but there is also a faint scent of lemon. I reach out before me and feel for the walls and discover a waxy-covered rope. I pull at it and the lemon scent intensifies. I feel around it and notice that the other ropes have a similar feel but whereas the lemon scented one is smooth, these are rough.

Taking a chance, I follow the smooth lemon scented rope and let it lead me around twists and turns. I feel like it's taking me from one side of the web to the other but finally I tumble through a hole and hit the ground. I blink, realizing I'm free of the web and sprint toward the flag. I collapse in a heap one second before the timer blares.

"Holy shit that was hard," I say aloud to no one in particular and remain on the ground.

"That was awesome, Ember," Kai says, walking up to me. "I knew you would figure it out. Okay, up you go. You're sparring with me first."

"Can I have like one minute?" I ask, forcing myself up.

He shakes his head. "No. If you're out on the field trying to rescue someone, will you have a minute to spare for rest?"

I glower at him. "No."

He nods. "That's my point. Now let's go. We're going to start out with the katanas."

"Do I really need to know how to use every weapon?" I ask, follow-ing him to a rack of weapons.

"Absolutely. You don't have to master each one, but you need to be able to use a wide variety. You never know what situation you'll be in and when," Kai lectures.

"Kai, I think you're being a little pushy about this," I say, stopping before the rack and placing my hands on my hips.

He turns and looks me up and down. "I want you to be prepared for anything. Ulric and Zeke agree with me on this. We've all seen you way to close to death's door for our comfort. Hell, if it wasn't for Zeke giving you his blood while you were in my arms after we rescued you from Greed, there's no telling if you would have lived. I won't see that happen again, Ember. I've waited for what feels like eternity to find you and I refuse to let you slip away."

I stare at Kai stunned and drop my arms to my side. I step forward and wrap my arms around him in a tight hug. "I will not come that close to death again. I'll try not to complain too much but remember, I'm already pushing myself a lot as it is."

He rubs his hands up and down my back. "I know you are. I just worry. Let's work on your use of the katana. Ulric is going to work with you and your wings. I haven't been having you do anything other than strengthening them, so hopefully he can get you in the air. He mentioned you were trying before."

I shrug. "Yeah, but we've already been doing so much and none of you have them, so I didn't really bring it up. I guess I could have asked Lucifer, but he's always so busy."

He shakes his head. "He stays busy. You'll work with Ulric on flying, starting today. Our small team is going to change quite a bit with Zeke and Ulric's training techniques added to our schedule."

"Oh, jeez, I better apologize to everyone then. I don't think their ready for that." I snort and Kai gives me the side-eye as we end our embrace.

"They'll be fine. Let's get a move on. Have you worked with one of these before?" He looks at the katana on the wall pointedly and I reach for it.

"A little. It's like the sword I carry with me regularly only the katana is lighter." I hold the katana in my hand, gently glancing it over.

"We will practice with it, then I'll have you move on to work with Ulric. Zeke is working on agility with everyone individually. I may have him do more of a group thing next time." Kai sounds contemplative.

"Just don't make Vixie and I late to work with Minerva. Her spell work is difficult for us, and I know she's going to be just as tired as I am from our spell yesterday." I groan and follow Kai to a training platform.

"I won't keep you past that time. We'll do this for a short period before you work with Ulric."

I nod at his words, and he catches me off guard as he launches toward me. I move the katana, blocking him and surprising myself. It moves so much easier than my usual weapon. Kai spins and swings lower, attempting to catch me off guard. I know he won't actually cut me if he makes it past my sword, but the fear is still there.

We circle each other around the mat, taking turns moving in to engage the other. He seems to be taking it somewhat easy on me as we move, and it lets me adapt better to the katana's weight. I feel like I could switch it out and use it rather than the sword I've been using.

After a good thirty minutes, with aching arms and legs, Kai calls for a break. I place the katana back on the rack and he has everyone rotate. I grudgingly move toward Ulric who smiles at me.

"Are you ready to fly, little wolf?" he asks as I stop before him.

I nod enthusiastically, ignoring my fatigue, and start stretching out my wings. They ache from not being used as much but they feel stronger.

"Good. Start with those and then we're going to move into working to lift you off the ground. Kai said you've been strengthening them with your conditioning." Ulric moves in circles around me, watching me loosen up.

"Yes. They feel stronger than they were before. Hopefully, I can get a little airtime."

He nods and watches me finish my stretching. "First thing I want you to do is flap them, trying to lift off the ground. I want you to practice using them to hover in place. Once you've accomplished that, we can try more."

I frown but stretch my white wings wide. I move them gently in the motion I desire before adding more force. I tense my jaw, pushing power into them and I feel them lift me off the ground. My eyebrows shoot up in shock as I glance at the ground a few feet under me. "Holy shit, I'm in the air," I exclaim.

Ulric claps. "Very good. Now let's see how long you can maintain that."

"You mean like hover for as long as possible?"

He nods. "That's exactly what I mean."

I focus on my wings and time drifts by easily. My ability to stay airborne surprises me and I'm even more surprised when I finally lower to the ground and Ulric mentions that I was able to hold it for fifteen minutes solid.

"Wow, so can we try to fly now?" I ask expectantly.

"No, now we do it again. You have another forty-five minutes to go before you need to leave to work with Minerva, correct?" Ulric looks down at me.

I glance over at the large clock at the end of the field.

"Yes, that's right. Ugh. Can I try to fly tomorrow? Am I not going to work with Zeke?"

He smiles. "You're so impatient. Tomorrow after you work with Zeke, we'll fly. I'm taking up his time today whether he likes it or not to have you hover."

I huff. "I guess I can work with that." He laughs and I hoist myself back up into the air. My wings feel heavier this time and I know that I'm tiring. I manage to hover an entire thirty minutes before Kai dismisses Vixie and me.

"Oh my gosh, my wings feel like they're going to fall off now," I say as I stretch them out next to Ulric.

He chuckles. "That's part of it, little wolf. In no time at all, they'll be strong enough and used to the effort that they won't hurt like that. Only if you fly for extended periods of time will they be pretty sore. I've only had to do that a few times."

I grimace. "So basically be ready for that when the time comes?"

Ulric shrugs. "It probably won't hurt. As one of your mates, I'm going to make sure that you can handle everything. You've surprised me in many things your capable of already."

I roll my eyes. "We aren't talking about sex, are we? I mean I love talking about sex with you but right now?"

He shakes his head. "Go get ready to work your brain now. You don't need to be late."

I smile and move around to give each of my mates a peck on the cheek before leaving with Vixie. All three of them plan to work on their own training while I make my way through my lessons. I laugh when Leon and Blaze volunteer to work with them as Vixie and I head toward the estate. They almost seem starstruck now after working with them all morning. I know they have great insight on techniques so it could improve how deadly our group is overall.

Chapter 19

Time moves quickly when you have fun, at least that's what I tell myself as I sit before my vanity, preparing for the ball tonight. Arminda and I have been styling my hair and doing my makeup for the last two hours. I've been thankful for her help because she is capable of things I've only ever seen girls accomplish on *YouTube*.

My eyes are sultry with the smokey eyeshadow effect and lined with black mascara. She did a simple contour to make them pop even more and the blush she used on my cheeks looks regal. My lips are lined with a deep red and my hair is curled loosely where it will cascade down my shoulders.

"Okay, I think we're ready to get you into your dress. Put your heels on first though. It may be a challenge to get them on after." Arminda taps my shoulder as she spins across the bathroom to my long sapphire gown hanging on one of the towel hooks by the shower. It's covered in small beads that send light scattering across the room like diamonds. It's going to catch everyone's eye.

I lean down and pick up the sparkling silver heels resting next to my chair and begin to slide them on each foot, buckling the strap into place as soon as it feels comfortable. They shine as well when the light hits them.

Standing, I take a moment to adjust to the new angle my feet are at in the tall heels before walking toward Arminda in nothing but a slip. I pull it off as soon as I stop before her, and she helps me step into the dress. It fits like a second skin, and she zips it up before I turn to look at myself in the mirror across the room.

"Wow." I stare astonished at how different I look. It fits well and my wings make me look ethereal.

"You look beautiful, dear. Let me get your jewelry and then you can slide a few daggers into place. I made sure the fine pockets in your skirt had some as well. I doubt you'll have trouble tonight."

"I hope you're right, Arminda, but you can never be too prepared. The last ball kind of gave me a touch of PTSD." I shrug as she places a silver chain over my head. She then hands me matching earrings, bangles, and rings to slide on one at a time.

"I doubt anyone will harm you at this one. You have all three of your mates, your father, and many others guarding the estate. Anyone that would try to do anything would have to be an idiot." She shakes her head.

I let her twirl my hair some more and spray it with more hairspray as I contemplate the ball. Butterflies fill my belly, and I can't help but feel like something will happen tonight.

"There. You're all set. Now go out there and make sure your mates are ready." She smiles and I do the same before turning toward the door that leads to my room.

The guys have been hanging out in the sitting area all this time, waiting on me. They started getting ready about the same time I did, and I know it didn't take long for them to finish. I can only imagine what they've been doing while I've been busy with Arminda.

As I enter the room, the sight of the three of them steals my breath. Each of them has on a black tux with a sapphire vest beneath the jacket. They are dressed to the nines and my face breaks out into a smile. Zeke is reclined back with a book resting in his lap and a cup of red blood sitting on the coffee table in front of him. Ulric sits at the table with a book as well and Kai stands by the door, twirling his sword.

Feeling my gaze on them, they all three meet my eyes and smile. Each of them moves toward me with bright eyes. Zeke reaches me first and pulls me into his arms gently.

"You look gorgeous, love. I don't know if we should let you leave this room looking like that."

Ulric chuckles behind Zeke but Zeke maintains his hold around me. "I have to agree with Zeke. I think we should keep you here and ravish you."

Ever the voice of reason, Kai clears his throat. "You look lovely, Ember, but despite what your other mates say, we have to attend this ball." He scoots Zeke over roughly and pulls me out of his arms, causing me to laugh.

Kai wraps his arms around me and buries his face into the side of my neck, taking in my scent. "I know we have to attend," I state and he nips at my neck. Ulric growls, picking up the change in my scent as I respond to Kai's love bites.

"Your actions contradict your words, Kai." I feel Ulric snake his hands in around my waist and gently he tugs me from Kai.

"Okay, you guys," I say as Ulric wraps me in his arms. "As much as I enjoy the attention, I don't want you to mess up my dress or anything else. Arminda and I toiled away over my hair and makeup."

"We won't mess it up, little wolf," Ulric says deeply, placing a kiss behind my ear.

"Please step away from Ember before I'm forced to act. I have to put her crown on her before we go. I almost forgot." Arminda's voice snaps everyone to attention and Ulric steps back from me.

"I wouldn't have let them mess anything up, Arminda. We worked too hard on everything. Did you say crown?" I turn and gape at her a moment before I notice a box in her hand.

"Yes. Lucifer had one commissioned to match your dress." She opens the box and moves to stand before me. I glance down and spot an elegant silver crown with diamonds and sapphires inlaid into it. It sparkles as I pick it up from the box. It amazes me how heavy it is.

Arminda reaches up and gently takes it from me. I meet her gaze as she nods, and I tilt my head down. She lifts it up and I feel its weight rest on my head. She soothes my hair down around it and I meet her gaze as I adjust to this new weight.

"I know it feels heavier than it looks but with a crown comes a lot of responsibility as you've seen thus far. This is only the beginning for you, Ember. I hope you realize that," she whispers.

"I do, Arminda, and I'm thankful to have someone like you on my side in all of this." I reach forward and grab her hands and notice the tears she fights to hold at bay.

"Are we ready, ladies?" Kai asks, grabbing our attention.

I turn and glare at him, asking him silently to give us a moment longer. Kai smirks in response. "Can't you see we're having a moment here? Is it really that important for me to arrive on time at my own coming-out party?"

"Waiting on you is not the distraction and tardiness idea I had in mind. Plus, if we're going to be late, then I think we should do other things than what we're currently doing," Zeke declares.

"I'm with Zeke on that idea," Ulric adds.

I roll my eyes. "You guys know I've worked way too hard on what I have on and my appearance to just stop drop and roll around with you all. Let's go get this over with so we can go find my sisters."

"That's the spirit," Kai says as I walk toward him.

"Oh, hush it. Let's go." I shake my head with a smile.

Arminda walks at my side and Ulric and Zeke fall in behind us as Kai holds the door open. He offers me a sexy smile as I pass and enter the hall.

Arminda leads us through the estate slowly. I'm thankful she doesn't rush us as I pull myself together, putting on a confident air. It will hide the nerves and fear I have in facing all these new people. People that I may have to someday lead.

Stop worrying, little wolf. You can handle this, Ulric whispers down our connection and I feel the other two send love and encouraging emotions with his words.

Thanks. I don't want it to show that I'm nervous though. Someone may see that as a weakness. I keep my gaze forward, following Arminda as we near the hall where the ball will be held.

Being authentic and real is not a weakness, love. Never forget that. Show them you, not who you think they want to see. Zeke's words cause me to pause my thoughts and my steps falter briefly.

He has good advice. I think that would be the best method in moving forward, Kai chimes in.

I nod silently and stop behind Arminda as we stare at the doors that will grant us entry into the ball. A man in a tailored suit stands, waiting with a smile on his face. I know he is to announce us before we enter.

Arminda turns, offering me a smile as she reaches out to squeeze my hand. Then in a blink, she's moving away toward the man by the door and whispers in his ear.

The man nods then looks to us before turning and slipping through the door with Arminda. A moment later, I hear a trumpet sounding from the other side of the door and the doors swing open. I take a deep breath and step forward with my three mates at my back.

Entering through the door, I almost stagger at the brightly lit room and the amount of people gathered within. They all smile eagerly at me as

I move. I follow the only path open as it leads me toward the center of the room where Lucifer sits upon a throne. He has an elegant chair next to him with smaller chairs for my three mates situated to his left in a line. It takes up a lot of space on the platform on which he's seated but it distinguishes our place above the guests.

The room is decorated in various shades of blue and I let my gaze dance across it and its occupants as I slowly make my way down the aisle.

The tables are set with the finest of silver furnishings, the chandeliers glow, and food is piled along a table at the back wall. Even the paintings on the walls have been changed to match the theme of silver and blue.

I smile at the people I pass as they bow their heads. It makes me feel slightly awkward as I continue forward. I know in the back of my mind, this is going to be what my future holds. People will be beneath me but even so, they can still be treated fairly. Maybe that's something I can make sure happens moving forward.

As I reach the small steps leading to the dais where Lucifer sits, I smile up at him. I gently pick up my skirt and ascend slowly so as not to trip and fall. Lucifer takes my hand once I'm close and my mates move to the open chairs.

Lucifer turns me as he announces to the room, "Here she is, everyone. My daughter and heir to my throne. I present to you, Ember."

The room explodes with applause and cheers as my belly does a somersault. I scan the room and spot Greed and Alora standing to one side with Prospero and Edsel close by. Greed looks bored but I can't help but wonder what's behind his mask.

Lucifer releases my hand and I switch my attention back to him. "I also would like to formally introduce her three mates." I watch as Ulric, Kai, and Zeke step forward. "Many of you may recognize them I'm sure. I couldn't have picked better matches myself. I present Prince Ezekiel, of the vampires, Prince Ulric, son of my brethren, Greed, and finally, my strongest most fearsome warrior, General Kai."

I beam at the flattery Lucifer rained on my mates and feel our bonds sing with joy. Shouts of joy and applause drown out everything until Lucifer raises his hand again.

"Now that introductions have been made, you may dance and make merry. Enjoy the food." The crowd once again bursts my eardrums with cheers. Lucifer turns to me with a smile. "You look beautiful tonight, Ember. If you'll follow me, I would like to introduce you to some important people."

I nod. "What will my mates do? Will they join us?"

Lucifer chuckles and looks over my shoulder. "Men, why don't you mingle for a bit while I borrow Ember. I need to introduce her to the elites, all of whom you already know."

Lucifer ushers me forward and down the steps to a small group of individuals standing to the side. I recognize some of the faces from the portrait in Greed's gallery as we approach. Nerves dance in my belly as I catch Greed and Alora making their way toward the group as well. Will they bring up the fact that I was once in their home, or will they play dumb?

"Everyone, meet my heir," Lucifer announces as the group pauses and stares at me.

"Hi," I offer with a light wave, feeling awkward.

A woman with long dark hair and green eyes steps forward. I recognize her from somewhere but can't place her. "Hello, Ember, I'm Persephone. It's a pleasure to meet you. This is my love, Hades." She points to a man with long black hair laced with bits of blue. "Welcome to our world. I'm so glad the rumors we heard were true and Luc has an heir. He's like family to Hades and me."

Hade's laugh is deep as he steps forward and takes my hand. "Excuse my love's over excitement. We spend a lot of time at Luc's estate. She'll enjoy your presence. Welcome to our world." He places a light kiss on my wrist, and I look up at Persephone as she beams.

Another female steps forward. Her hair is the color of rainbows and shimmers when she moves. She wears a skintight dress, and her eyes are bright shades of purple. "Hi, Ember, I'm Lust. Where have you been hiding all this time? You're gorgeous."

Unsure of how I should answer, I glance over at Lucifer. He smiles and nods in encouragement.

I turn back to face her. "It's a long story so maybe another time we can talk about it?"

Lust laughs, and it sounds like music flowing through my ears. "I guess that's fine. It's hard to believe that you have been hidden for so long."

I smile but don't miss the flash of anger in her eyes before she regains her composure. I can't help but wonder what that was about.

The group shuffles a bit as Greed and Alora join. They wear matching shades of emerald and Alora even has a gorgeous emerald set of jewelry decked out across her form. Prospero remains back in the crowd behind them scowling. Alora smiles at me and Greed frowns in confusion.

Lucifer speaks up. "Ah, Greed, brother, how have you been?"

I place a smile on my face as the tension thickens in the air around us.

"Lucifer, you are looking magnificent as always. I have been well. Alora and I have been enjoying ourselves." Greed intones his head toward Lust. "I do believe we have her mother to thank for that."

Lust giggles. "She is every bit of me as any of my children."

"Yes, that is great. I hear you have been busy. How're you all enjoying the party thus far?" Lucifer asks the group.

"Oh, it is beautiful," Alora gushes. "I love the decor you chose!"

"Thank you for the compliment. Greed, are you pleased one of your sons is my daughter's mate?" Lucifer's rapid change in subject throws me for a loop but I watch intently as Greed schools his features into one of pleasant surprise.

"I am but I thought she was mated to Prospero to be honest. I guess I was wrong," Greed states.

"Is there a hidden story to this?" A large angel steps forward. His dark hair is pulled back into a braid and he holds himself proudly. His wings glisten as the light hits them. His stern expression doesn't match the curiosity in his eyes.

Lucifer chuckles. "This is Pride. I do believe my daughter spent some time at Greed's home."

I look between Lucifer and Greed, trying to gauge the feeling between them, but Lucifer looks smug while Greed appears bored. Is Greed concerned and hiding it? Is he worried that I shared his plans? Does he know that I know his plans?

"She did spend some time with us, yes. She had a fling with my son, Prospero. I thought it was headed somewhere but we see how that turned out." Greed's words are soft as if trying to make light of the situation.

"How nice." Another male steps forward. He's dark skinned with blond hair and grey eyes. He doesn't have wings, so it sparks my curiosity. "I do believe Ember looks bored. I'm Thanatos, darling, would you care to dance?"

"That would be wonderful," I respond and let him take my hand.

I glance over my shoulder and all three of my mates stand nearby. They are conversing with a group of partygoers, but Kai catches my eye and nods as if to say he'll be okay to dance with.

Feeling better having gotten confirmation that Thanatos is less likely to harm me or cause other issues, I turn my gaze back to him.

He winks and chuckles. "Seeking approval? You don't seem like the type to take orders from your mates."

I let out a nervous giggle. "I don't know a lot of these partygoers, having only spent a short amount of time here in Hell. Having them re-assure me in some things helps. Should they not have approved that you wouldn't cause me trouble?"

"Of course not, dear. You're in safe hands. I try not to cause trouble too often." He laughs and I smile at his words.

"I see that you don't have wings. I'm still learning about the various individuals who maintain residence here. Are you like what Persephone and Hades are?"

Thanatos spins me into motion as we step onto the dance floor. Soft gentle jazz is playing, and other dancers move gracefully around the floor. I follow his lead, having never danced to this before and he seems to pick up on my concern.

He finally nods and answers my question. "Somewhat, yes. I do work with them in the underworld. I'm generally one to receive the souls when its time, so I go back and forth a lot. The job is quite tiring, really."

I frown as we continue dancing. "I imagine that must be difficult."

"It is. The souls are very confused at first, after death. Once they have been through the judgment with Hades, they tend to be more relaxed. Well, most of them anyway. Of course, I only take those with Greek origins or those who believe in the gods and goddesses associated with the Greeks. There are many divisions like that in this realm. Even Lucifer has his sec-tion. If you're interested, maybe we can get together sometime, and I can teach you about our realm?"

"I would have to get back to you on that. I don't know what my schedule is like off the top of my head. Maybe you could speak with my tutor, Arminda? That sounds like a fascinating topic."

"What have you learned thus far?" he asks curiously.

"Well, I've learned quite a bit about Hell, but that's it." I shrug.

"So, you don't know all the history yet? Where were you hiding?" He lifts a brow in curiosity.

"Earth, so no. I have a lot to catch up on. Arminda is an excellent tutor and so is Minerva."

He beams. "That is fascinating."

A hand lands on Thanatos's shoulder, drawing our attention and causing us to stop. A deep voice that I instantly recognize meets my ears before my gaze lands on him.

"May I cut in?" Prospero asks from behind Thanatos.

I stiffen as Thanatos steps back from me and bows, bending lightly at the waist. "Of course, my friend. Ember, it was a pleasure. I'll see you again soon."

I nod as Prospero steps forward and pulls me toward him gently. His touch is familiar but softer than it was before. "Don't you look lovely tonight, Princess. You know, I do have half a mind to steal you away but that would be difficult. Your mates are already glaring holes through me. I wonder how long they'll let us dance?"

"You would be very stupid to attempt to take me away from here. I'm honestly surprised you came tonight. I didn't think you or your father would show."

"I couldn't miss the opportunity to see the woman I love again, now could I? Even if you are tied to my brother and two others." He lets out a deep sigh. "I also wanted to make amends. You opened a new side of me that has been closed off since my mother's death. It's painful, but I've realized that I've done a lot of bad things in my life."

"So, what are you trying to say?" I ask skeptically.

"I guess I'm trying to apologize for the things I've done to you."

"That's surprising. I'm impressed you are honestly apologizing right now."

"Well, you did leave quite the impression on me."

"Does this mean you'll stop trying to create an army and treating other women as toys?" I lift my brow as I look at him glancing up and down.

"I am going to try to curb those habits, yes, but it will take some time. It's not like I can walk away from it all. I do intend to move forward with my father in the attack. Hell needs something different, a new role, or someone to fix things, because the way they currently are, is not working."

I frown. "I don't understand why you wish to do that. War brings more trouble than it's worth. Death and destruction. I just don't get it."

Prospero lightly shrugs while scanning everyone around us. "Maybe one day you'll understand."

"Brother." Ulric's voice comes from behind me, and I step away from Prospero before turning to face my mate.

"Ulric. I see you've recovered from your spell," Prospero sneers.

"I have, yes. If you'll excuse me, I'd like to dance with my mate." Ulric's voice drops deeper, and I can hear the hidden threat. I was curious as to how long they would let me and Prospero dance before intervening. Now I know.

"Of course. Ember, love, I'll see you soon." Prospero bows lightly and I feel the tension radiating off Ulric behind me.

"Later," I respond before he walks off.

Ulric grabs my hand and pulls me closer to him, planting a kiss on my lips, and claiming me in front of everyone in the room. It must reassure him. The music changes to something slower and we began to move.

"I really can't stand him touching you. What did he say to you?" Ulric's expression is hard, and I can see the anger toward his brother simmering at the surface.

"Mostly he apologized and said he would try to be better, but not to the point he would push to halt your father's vendetta against Lucifer."

"Of course not. Why would he turn his back on what my father wants? That takes more courage than he has, more guts."

I nod, listening to my mate rant. I get it though, all the feelings toward Prospero.

We continue to dance as the night progresses, and I switch from dancing with him to my other mates. After the dance with Prospero, they've been a bit more protective, not allowing anyone else to dance with me. I did get to chat with more of Lucifer's friends and thankfully, I was able to easily escape later in the night.

As soon as my mates and I enter the hall outside the ballroom, I stop and pull off my heels. "Oh my God, my feet hurt so bad. I've never danced that much for that long in heels."

Zeke grabs the heels from my hands as he chuckles. "I wondered how long you would last wearing those."

Deep laughter rolls around me as I roll my eyes. "Yes, well, I made it. I'm pretty sure Arminda would have had my head had I not worn them."

Kai laughs even louder. "Probably."

We grow silent and my thoughts begin to dance around my head as I think of what tomorrow may bring. Sensing my thoughts, Ulric asks, "Care to share with the group what's going on up there?"

I let out a deep sigh. "I was just thinking about what we will do first tomorrow. How will we start our journey to find my sisters?"

Kai steps closer and takes my hand. "We'll start from my uncle's place and see what the scouts have for us. Once we have a plan, we'll go from there."

"How will we get there though? I haven't even thought of that," I exclaim.

Ulric exchanges a look with Zeke before speaking. "Zeke and I have that covered. We're going to travel with Absalom and the rest of the vampires for a time before making our way on our own."

"Oh," I say, making a big O with my mouth.

Zeke taps my chin. "Better close that before you catch a fly or something. Come on, let's go get some rest. We have a busy day tomorrow."

Chapter 20

Yawning, I roll over in bed, reaching an arm out as I do. Finding the mattress empty, I jolt into sitting and blink, trying to wake up. Ulric's chuckle to my left causes me to whip around.

I rub my eyes. "What time is it?"

He moves toward me and sits at the end of the bed. "It's six a.m. We're packing up some stuff to take with us on our journey. Do you want to sleep more? I can pack for you."

I shake my head. "Thanks, but no. I want to be alert when we move out. I do want to call my parents though before we leave."

Ulric nods. "I'm going to finish up and head out front. Zeke and Kai have already left to help the vampires load and make sure the others will be ready. Don't forget to put on your armor. It's better to wear it rather than pack it. Easier to travel that way."

"Should I pack light then?"

"Yes. Only what's necessary."

"Right. I should know that. Okay, I'll touch base with my parents." I stand from the bed and Ulric gives me a quick kiss. I smile when he moves away and busy myself, digging the compact mirror out of my drawer.

It's warm when I pull it out, almost as if someone has been trying to get through to me. Worry spikes in my chest as I flip it open and stare at the mirrored surface before me. Did something happen while the ball was taking place last night?

I close my eyes and feel my magic stir to life as the mirror tingles in my hands. Opening them, I find it filled with a swirling mist before Adam and Corey's faces appear. I arch a brow as I wait to see if my parents will come through and see the guys frown.

"I don't think your dad will show up this morning," Corey says somberly.

"Why, did something happen?" I ask, sitting back on the bed.

Adam nods his head. "We were attacked last night by a large group of various creatures. Some were Imps and others, well, I'm not sure what to call them. Everyone in the pack went on the defensive to defend the land. They've taken up new roles in keeping the pack safe and well. Ember, I hate to tell you this, but your mother didn't make it. She was killed while fighting."

I stare into the mirror, stunned at Adam's words. My mother can't be gone. She just can't. It's impossible. Pain slices through me and I fight the urge to scream. This can't be true. How will my sisters handle this? How are we going to move forward?

"We're sorry, Ember," Corey adds and tears stream down my cheeks.

"Is she really gone?" I ask softly, trying to pull myself together. I need to be strong.

Adam sighs sadly. "Yes, darling. I'm so sorry. The attack shocked us all. Your mother fought bravely. She had even been helping with the stuff for the elder council. She was searching for those that may have had a part in what my father has been into."

Something in Adams words made me pause. "Did your dad plan the attack on our pack? Would he do that to his own people?"

Corey shrugs as Adam grunts. "I wouldn't put it past him. We've seen that he has an ulterior agenda. Maybe this was part of it. The elder council is probably on its way now to investigate. I reported the attack to them, and it got through quickly. I guess we'll find out soon."

Anger surges through me and I feel all my mates through our connection. They focus in on my emotions, but I ignore it. "I'll personally kill your father, Adam, if he had something to do with this."

Many emotions flit across Adam's face as my words sink in. "I won't stand in your way if you do. He may be my father, but he has betrayed all of us."

Tears continue to stream from my eyes as I smile wickedly. "Good."

The door bursts open, and I jerk my head up, dropping the mirror in surprise as all three of my mates enter the room. They begin searching around for an attacker as I pick up the mirror with a confused Corey and Adam in it.

"What just happened, Em?" Corey asks.

Ulric moves closer to me and looks down at the mirror. "We thought she was being attacked. Her emotions spiked and it wasn't pleasant."

I pull Ulric to me and set the compact down on the side table as Zeke and Kai move closer to us. "My pack was attacked, and my mother was killed. I think Alpha Gale may be behind it."

"Shit, she's dead?" Zeke asks, moving next to me on the bed and wrapping me in a hug.

"She was killed while defending us, Zeke," Corey adds.

"She was a beautiful and talented woman, Ember. She'll be missed. I hate this for you. Have you already buried her body?" Zeke turns his attention to Adam and Corey.

"They did it first thing this morning. We unfortunately had quite a few losses," Adam says sadly.

"After we retrieve Ember's sisters, we'll help in whatever way we can to strengthen the defenses," Ulric says and Kai grunts in agreement behind me.

"I appreciate that, gentlemen. We may need it to wrangle my father. The council will also be involved. We had to report the attack to them this morning." Adam continues to frown.

"This is not good. We will do what we can to be quick. I'm not sure what shape the girls will be in or what we'll be walking into. We'll join you as soon as we can though and help with the council," Zeke suggests.

"When will the council arrive?" I wipe at my eyes and stare at my friends.

"We're not sure but we can try to keep you updated. Take the mirror with you to retrieve your sisters and contact us as soon as they're safe. I'll try to get your dad to call you. He's not doing so well right now." Corey rubs his forehead as the stress seems to settle on him.

"Thanks, Corey. I'm going to let you guys go. The quicker we get moving, the quicker we can make it up to help there. I'm bringing my sisters home." We all say goodbye and I close the mirror. My mates hug me before leaving to help finish preparation for the trip.

I take a little more time to finish packing than I had originally planned to do as I try to process all the emotions behind the news of my mother's death. It doesn't seem real. I make sure the mirror is snuggled into my bag with all the necessary items before throwing it over my shoulder. Everything feels heavy as I move toward the door. Why must life be so challenging?

I fight back tears as I continue to make my way down the hall and to the front of the estate. Part of me wants to go back to my room and curl into a ball beneath the covers. I want to pretend that this is all a dream. I know I can't though because my sisters' lives depend on me. My mother wouldn't want me to mourn like that. She would want me to keep living, to fight, and to keep those we love safe.

The grief is so heavy and feels crushing. How do I box it up and ignore it? Is there a way to just push it off?

Anger surges through me at the hopelessness in dealing with my grief. It's uncalled for but my hands warm and I want to scream. Instead, I pull my strap on my pack closer to my shoulder and grit my teeth. Once I find my sisters, those who have them are going to feel my wrath.

The strange light of the unusual sky in Hell blinds me as I push through the front door of the estate. The sight of many dragons greets me as I stop on the porch. Their beautiful scales glisten and steam rises from their noses. They seem happy.

Several of the vampires move around, tightening harnesses and bags, preparing for the departure. They seem so carefree, just like I was not too long ago. I let out a heavy sigh as I make my way toward Zeke as he stands before an enormous purple dragon. It has white claws and its eyes twinkle as I approach.

"Hey, love." He steps forward and wraps his arms around me. "You're going to be riding with me on this lovely beast. She's mine."

"Cool. She is very pretty. I love her color." At my words, the dragon moves its long neck and brings its snout right up to me as if asking to be petted.

Zeke laughs. "She seems to like you. I'm glad."

I tentatively reach out a hand and rest it on her snout. Her scales are firm and smooth. She snorts and a puff of smoke comes through her nose. "I guess that means you like me?"

She nods her head up and down and I pull my hand back with a small laugh. She moves it back to face forward as Zeke grabs my bag off my shoulder and tosses it up into the saddle resting on her back.

"Do you need a boost up, love?" Zeke runs a hand through his hair as he stares at me.

"I think I got it. I do have wings you know, and I can use them." I smirk at him and use my wings to glide up to the saddle.

Zeke snorts and joins me. "Get comfortable, dear, this is going to be a long flight."

I roll my eyes and wrap my arms around Zeke. The ride can't be too bad, can it?

I freeze as the dragon's muscles tense beneath us, and gasp as she launches into the air. My stomach drops and I'm momentarily shocked at how fast we're moving. I lean over the side and watch the ground disappear. It's much different from flying in a plane and strangely I feel more comfortable sitting on a dragon. Is it because it's a living being, and I don't trust technology? I'm not sure, but as we rise higher and higher, I feel a warmth settle around me.

Confused, I glance over Zeke's shoulder at the dragon's head and see a scale glowing on its head.

Zeke chuckles. "Dragons have their own magic. She's creating a warm shield around us so we don't freeze. It's nice, isn't it?"

I squeeze him tighter and rest my head against his shoulders as I respond. "It is. I think I need to spend more time learning about them. Why doesn't Lucifer have any?"

"Oh, I'm sure he does somewhere. He's the ultimate ruler here, so why wouldn't he?"

"I don't know. I just haven't come across any. I'll have to find out. I would love to have my own."

The ride isn't too bad, and I find myself dozing off on occasion. The emotional high of the morning has faded and fatigue has replaced it. How am I going to tell my sisters the news? I squeeze my eyes tight as another round of tears tries to surface. I'll figure this all out. One step at a time.

Chapter 21

Hours later, we land in a large field near a dusty road. It's just wide enough for a few of the dragons to land in. Our group quickly dismounts with weapons and bags. Vixie smiles as she bounces up to me full of excitement.

"That was absolutely amazing, wasn't it? I always love riding dragons."

I smile at her and nod. "Maybe we can do it again some time." I turn to Kai as he walks up. "Is it far to your uncles?"

He looks at the tree line and then at the sky. "It shouldn't be. Maybe an hour or two walk? It's hard to judge from here. I don't usually travel via dragon."

"Yeah, we usually just run it," Vixie says with a shrug.

Ulric walks up to our small group with his bag thrown over his shoulder. "I'm sure we can make it in no time at all. Some of us could run and others could fly."

"I'm in for a run," Zeke adds.

Blaze and Leon walk up, smiling as if they had just finished sharing a joke with each other.

"We could go for a run as well." Blaze smiles and winks at me.

"Yeah, my legs are cramped up from the ride," Leon agrees.

Kai grunts. "I guess it's settled then. We'll move quickly. I'll stay in the lead so just follow me. Ulric, are you going to fly? Ember, are you running or flying?"

"Of course, I'll fly. I'm definitely not walking if you're all running."

I roll my eyes. "I'll run. I don't think my wings will get me there as easily as Ulric's. I still have a way to go in strengthening them. Plus, I enjoy letting my hound loose."

"Well, now that we all know how we're traveling, let's get moving." Kai turns and begins his transformation. His giant hellhound replaces his human-like figure seconds later.

I smile at his hound form and then start my own transformation. My magic swirls through me, filling me with warmth, before my limbs elongate and my face changes. Soon, I stand on all fours with my tail wagging.

Kai breaks out into a sprint, and I follow. I hear the others behind me, but my inner hound seems to think this is a game and I race after my mate.

I dart down the trail as the wind breezes through my fur. It's rejuvenating and a piece of me feels free. It's almost as if all the thoughts and emotions I had in my human form are gone now that I breeze over the dirt as a hellhound.

In what seems like no time at all, I spot a large estate on a hill in the distance. It's lit brightly as evening descends.

As we grow closer, the trail becomes cleaner as if someone maintains it. Kai comes to a stop, and we do as well.

We're almost there. Around a few more bends and we'll be at the gate. We'll move at a slower pace now.

I nod my head and ruffle my fur as I take off at a trot behind Kai. Moving slower lets me take in how dense the forest is around us and how green everything is. It reminds me of home in spring when everything begins to bud and burst with life again. It's so beautiful.

As we continue forward, Kai leads us through an elaborate gate minutes later. Green vines dance up the side of the stone structure with pink flowers blooming all over. It reminds me of something from a regency novel or movie. The white stone behind the plants makes their color pop.

The sound of light footfalls drags my attention from thoughts of the gate, and I perk up my ears as I glance around us. There is a massive open space between the gate and the huge estate. It's equivalent to three football fields and is excellent for running.

An enormous three-headed dog pads toward us from the front of the house. All three of its tongues loll out to the side and its short tail wags violently. It lets out an excited yip which causes me to tilt my head.

Kai yips back at him and the two run toward each other. Kai pounces on him. The bigger dog rolls him over and pins him to the ground. I let out a wolfish laugh and walk up toward the two as they continue to wrestle. I sit back on my haunches, watching them until they shift back into their main forms.

Cerberus chuckles as he stands, shaking his long hair side to side. "I'm glad you guys made it. I've been watching all day to see when you would arrive. I take it everything went okay at the ball last night, Ember?"

I call my power forward and let it wash over me, returning to my own form, wings, and all. "It did, although I didn't get the best of news this morning. My mother was killed in an attack on my pack."

Cerberus frowns. "I'm sorry to hear that, Ember. How are you handling it?"

I feel Zeke and Ulric as they rest a hand on my shoulder. "I'm handling it as best as I can, given the circumstances. I'm not sure how things are going to be, moving forward."

Kai moves forward to pull me into his arms. "We will all be here as we move forward together." He releases me and turns back to Cerberus. "Uncle, have you heard any news of our scouts?"

Cerberus nods his head. "Yes, they are on patrol again tonight but reported they will come tomorrow to fill us in on the details. The twins anyway. The others will remain behind. They found a cabin in the woods not too far from the gate to Heaven."

"Is that good or bad that they're so close to the gate?" I ask.

"It's not necessarily good or bad, honestly. If my father is planning to try to break through the gate, then we have another pile of shit to add to his desire to take over Hell." Ulric groans.

"I wouldn't put it past him, Ulric. He is Greed after all," Zeke chimes in.

"Well, whatever his plans are, we need to do our best to figure them out, but handle what we came to do first. We need more proof before we act on him trying to take out the gate," Kai suggests.

"Wait, does my father have access to the gate? Can he open it?" I ask hesitantly.

"Yes of course he can. He's Lucifer," Kai says with an eye roll, growing tired of the conversation.

"If Greed is already planning to attack my father, what would stop him in planning something for after?"

Zeke groans. "I guess that would make sense."

Cerberus huffs. "Greed seems to have been planning this for a long time. Let's go in and get you guys something to eat before we talk about this further."

Everyone walks at a leisurely pace to the house, carrying their bags. Now that I'm no longer in my hellhound form, I feel exhaustion weigh on me. It's been one long day.

Cerberus leads us up to a large set of steps before a huge stone estate. It's white with dark blue trim and window shutters. The vegetation around it is immaculate and I can tell it's well taken care of.

He pushes through a large set of double doors and leads us down the hall. He points out the dining room, a tearoom, lounge room, and several others before leading us up a set of spiral stairs at the back of the house. They open to a quiet carpeted floor lined with doors. I love how soft the carpet looks and its dark grey color. It makes me feel calm especially with the faint blue painted walls lining each side.

Cerberus leads us to each door, announcing whose room is whose, and we drop our things off before he gives us a tour of the rest of the house. There are rooms on the next level for the maids, butlers, and any other helpers residing on the residence. He mentions that there is also a separate building behind the house that offers larger rooms for families if they wish to live there.

He leads us up to another floor, the top and final floor, and mentions that this is where his quarters are located as well as any other family members who choose to stay on the estate. Many of them live in different areas of the realm though, leaving the watching of Heaven's gate to Cerberus himself.

Soon, we're all seated at the dining table with steaming food before us, wine, and other delights. I immediately pick up the wine and toss it back once my glass has been filled. The butler eyes me as I set it down.

As he tilts his head to the side, I ask, "Can you go ahead and top it off?"

He nods and fills it to the top before moving down the table. I pick up the glass and sip on it this time. I look up and meet Zeke's curious gaze and shrug. It's not like I need to explain what's happening inside. They've all heard everything I have today. It doesn't sit the same on their shoulders as it does mine.

I glance at the butler as he returns with the bottle of wine and sets it next to my glass now resting on the table. He winks before walking off and

I hear Ulric snort down the table.

I look at him confused. "What?"

"Dandelion thinks you may need more, apparently." Cerberus chuckles. "He's been one of my favorite assistants for years. He can pick up on the emotions of others and you obviously confirmed what he felt. He'll probably be back with another, my dear, just for you."

"Would it be bad if I drank more? After all, we're going to fight to get my sisters back tomorrow, right?"

Kai shakes his head. "We won't know what our plan is until we talk with the scouts. You know you won't get drunk as easy since you've shifted."

"I won't?"

Zeke laughs. "She hasn't had a chance to really test it out, Kai. I don't think tonight would be a bad night to temporarily drown out your problems."

"I don't think it's a good idea. Do what you're comfortable with though, little wolf. We get it if you want to indulge." Ulric purses his lips and I feel concern radiating across his connection to me.

I frown, staring down at my glass and the bottle next to it. Yes, it would make the feelings go away but it would be temporary. Would they hit harder when they came back? How much would be too much?

"I think I'm going to take it easy. I don't want to get hammered. I know I'm feeling a lot right now, but with great power comes great responsibility, right?" I ask with a shrug.

"You know everyone who says that in the movies dies, right?" Zeke asks with a brow raised.

"I'll be fine. It's a great tip to follow. I'm ready to get things moving forward and find a way to help my pack. I know I need to work on things in this realm as well, but we have more time here than they do there."

"Don't stress about it, Ember. You'll get it all done. If you're anything like your father, your determination will help you there," Cerberus says, sipping at his glass.

"Do we have an idea of what we might be facing?" Ulric clears his throat.

"Somewhat." Kai sips at his wine. "We know that the group working with Stole is holed up in a cabin surrounded by a lot of vegetation. The forest will give us great coverage when moving in for the attack."

"The last I heard from them is that they aren't sure about the number of individuals they have there, both captive and assisting Stole. Many have gone in and out, but it's been difficult to tell. I hope the scouts will have a better idea when they come tomorrow." Cerberus swirls the wine in his glass as he speaks.

"So, going into rescue would probably be best under the cover of darkness? I wonder if they are more active during the day versus the night?" Zeke muses.

"I guess we'll find out in the morning," Ulric declares.

I pick at my food while I listen to the conversation, as it changes from the topic of the cabin, to a lighter one. They begin sharing stories from their past. It gives me a chance to zone out and muse over my thoughts and feelings. I'm tired from the day but not ready to go to bed. At least I don't want to. I feel amped up, but not, at the same time.

I startle when Ulric's hand lands on my shoulder. I blink and take in the others' concerned faces around the table.

"How about I take you up to bed?" Ulric gently squeezes his hand.

I push out of my chair slowly. "That's probably for the best. Goodnight, everyone. I'll see you in the morning."

Ulric drops his hand from my shoulder to my elbow and guides me closer. He wraps his arm around my waist as he leads me from the room. We walk in silence down the hall and up the stairs to our room.

The bed seems to beckon me as I enter, and without thought, I begin stripping off my clothes and climb into the bed. I hear Ulric chuckle lightly, but he doesn't say anything as he climbs in next to me. Feeling comfortable, I curl up on his chest and unleash the tears that have been kept barely at bay all day.

Chapter 22

My head feels heavy as I sit at the dining table for breakfast. I slept hard after crying myself to sleep. I know that's why my head hurts so bad this morning. Crying will do that.

"The scouts should be here soon," Cerberus announces as he enters the room. He looks refreshed.

I grunt and sip at my coffee as Kai says from beside me, "Excellent. I can't wait to hear what they have to share. Should we convene in another room to discuss this with them?"

Ulric and Zeke remain quiet and watchful, as I hold my cup of coffee, feeling half asleep still.

"I'll have them come into the blue room and have refreshments brought in. I'm sure they are starving." Cerberus glances at me and the death grip I have on my cup. He assesses my eyes as well. "I'll also make sure there is fresh coffee."

"The blue room is the one at the back of the house, right?" Ulric asks, picking up a scone from the middle of the table.

"Yes, it overlooks the garden. It's also larger and we'll all fit within. Can someone notify the others in your party that we'll be there? I know they've wanted to keep to themselves so far, but I want us all to hear this information firsthand." Cerberus frowns.

"I can do that. It'll take me no time at all. How long do we have?" Zeke stands from his chair and rushes to give me a peck on the cheek.

"An hour, give or take." Cerberus scratches his head.

"I'll see you down the hall then." Zeke breezes out of the room.

I pick up another of the mini quiches and toss it into my mouth. I gorged on them while I waited for my coffee to cool but having a little more never hurts. They're full of protein so why not?

I feel Kai's eyes on me. "Come on, Ember. Let's go down the hall and get comfortable. I'll have Dandelion bring the remainder of the food down."

I nod and stand from my chair. I'm not awake enough yet to talk much. I know I slept hard, but it didn't take away the heavy feeling of losing my mother.

Ulric rests a hand on my back as we follow Kai and Cerberus down the hall. Cerberus branches off to go down another hall as Kai leads us the rest of the way. We enter and head toward one of the couches. I continue to hold my mug as I take in the room.

I purse my lips as I take in everything and just how blue it truly is. Now I know why they call it the blue room. The carpet is a dark navy blue that matches the heavy curtains. The furniture is a light sky blue, and the coffee table has a light blue lace overlay across its silver surface.

The couch looks like one you would find in an old lady's sitting room but is quite comfy. I lean back into its cushions amazed by its comfort. Ulric sits next to me and our wings brush against each other, sending comforting warmth through me. Ever my rock.

A short time later, after Dandelion brought in fresh coffee and food, Cerberus leads the twin scouts in. They look slightly haggard as if they haven't slept well in some time and dirt covers their clothes. They plop down on one of the many chairs in the room and grab a coffee.

The female, after sipping her cup of coffee, introduces herself. "Hello, I'm Mikai. It's a pleasure to finally meet you, Ember. This is my brother, Marley." She motions to the male beside her.

I take in their matching hair and eyes but other than that, the two are very different. Marley has a darker skin tone while Mikai's is lighter. Both are gorgeous and have muscle for days. Marley is about a foot taller than Mikai though.

"It's a pleasure to meet you as well, Ember. We know the others in the room. So, to get straight to it," Marley switches his gaze to Kai, "we found them."

I let out a breath, not realizing I had been holding it. "Are they okay? What kind of condition are they in? Will it be easy to get them away?"

Mikai holds up her hand. "Slow down, dear. We only caught a glimpse of them. They, as well as several other females, are being kept in cages inside the cabin basement. Guards are constantly on duty, going in and out, but Stole left a few days ago and hasn't returned yet. My brother and I think tonight may be the best time to move in and rescue them all."

"How many captives do they have exactly?" Kai asks in his authoritative voice.

Marley scratches his brow. "We couldn't get a set number but it's quite a few. I guess they've been bringing them here for some time."

"Do you know when they started that?" Ulric muses.

"Possibly a year or so ago. Locals report that it started happening about the time the gate near Greed's place exploded. They said it was when Heaven's portal rippled purple, which you know is when a gate is destroyed or permanently closed," Marley replies.

"Do you think they kept capturing women even after we rescued the others?" I direct my gaze to Ulric.

"It almost sounds like it," Zeke says.

"That's not good news," Vixie says, entering the room with the rest of our crew behind her. "Sorry we're late."

"Someone didn't want to wake up. Blaze glares at Leon who shrugs in response.

"Can you shut up so they can go back to sharing information please?" Vixie groans at Blaze.

Marley chuckles. "We missed you guys, too. They are keeping the captives in the basement. We were only able to slip in for a short time. It wasn't easy and the conditions they're keeping them in is horrible. They are all in rough shape."

"Shit. Are my sisters alive at least?" I ask, feeling rage spiral in me at what they've been through.

"They are," Mikai says softly. "A lot of the other women are not, and their bodies remain where they fell. It's bad."

"Are there more living or dead?" Leon asks, as he munches on one of the coffee cakes from the table.

"It's hard to say." Marley shrugs.

Cerberus growls. "Either way, we'll get all the living ones out to safety. Once we do that, we can figure out what to do about the deceased. We may not be able to get them and figure out who they are. The living are more important."

A chorus of agreements and nods come from everyone in the room while I sit quietly. Those poor girls.

"When will we move?" Vixie picks up her cup of coffee and takes a sip as she eyes the room.

"We'll leave this evening before dusk. That way we can make our way through the trees to spots surrounding the cabin. We can take any outer guards out before we move in. We'll need to be as discreet as possible," Kai commands, and I can feel the energy in his voice.

"Like that will be hard. You did bring the best." Vixie sets her cup down and crosses her arms as she rolls her eyes.

Kai growls as Leon and Blaze snicker. It seems they've had this conversation before. I feel a little lighter listening to them as they begin to banter.

"So, what do we need to do to prepare? Unlike you all, this is my first time." I shrug and they get quiet.

"You need to bring your A game, love. That's all. I think your instincts will take over. Just don't lose your head." Zeke smiles at me reassuringly.

"Why would I lose my head?" I stare at Zeke with my brow raised.

"Love, I've been around you for years. I know how you are when your family is involved. You're going to be volatile." Zeke chuckles.

I respond by flipping him the bird with a glare and standing to my feet. "Okay, for real. What do I need to do?"

Ulric walks to me and places a calming hand on my shoulder. "Just be ready for anything like you've been training for."

Kai grunts in agreement. "Everyone rest up and be ready to leave this evening. You'll all need to be energized. Mikai, Marley, take a bath. I'll see you all tonight. You're all dismissed."

I feel the need to yell "break" and clap my hands together at Kai's words but refrain. That is obviously a human thing, and they don't do it when having serious conversations. I plop myself back on the sofa after everyone but my mates leave.

Cerberus mumbles something about needing to reach out to a few other hellhounds in the area for backup and to retrieve the healers so they can help when we return. I love how confident he is, and it seems to bolster mine as well. He nods briefly in farewell to us as he leaves.

Kai takes a seat across from me. "Ember, do you have any questions about how this will go tonight? Do you want to talk anything over that's happened in the last twenty-four hours?"

I refill my cup of coffee and take a sip. It doesn't taste as great as usual because I didn't add creamer, but I don't care at this point. Hell, I may have to force myself to nap before tonight. I'm so tired. "No. I just want to get my sisters back and get this stuff with my pack figured out."

"Well, you can't go in with that attitude. Will you be able to focus? I can help guide you in this but you're going to have to listen to me," Kai says soothingly.

I growl in response, eliciting a chuckle from Ulric. "I'll listen."

Kai rolls his eyes. "Good. Go get some rest, love, before we go later. If you want, we can all come up and stay with you while you rest for a bit. My uncle will need me soon though to help get things organized."

I let out a sigh and push the frustration, anger, and other roiling emotions, threatening to rise in my fatigued state. "I would appreciate that."

Chapter 23

Crickets chirp and the wind whispers through the tops of the trees as our small band hides out in the brush surrounding the cabin. We took care of the few guards stationed in the trees upon arrival. Mikai and Marley hide closest to the cabin. Kai wants them to be the first to enter and give us the all clear.

My muscles cramp as I remain crouched beneath a giant bush. I've been in this position for hours, only moving my tail on occasion. All communication has been done telepathically, and we used a bottled potion, sent by Minerva, to help mask our scents. It was a strange green liquid that she thankfully put in a spray bottle. We were able to mist ourselves with it before shifting and it carried over.

The lights in the cabin dim, catching my attention. Does that mean the guards within are going to bed or is the night watch taking over? Is there even a night watch?

My muscles twitch as my magic swirls within, eager for me to unleash it on my sisters' captors. I know that if I can't rein myself in, I'll give us away.

Marley and Mikai, are you moving in? Kai's voice whispers through everyone's connection.

Mikai's voice sounds light as she responds, *Yes. We'll report shortly.*

I watch as the shadows move near where Mikai and Marley hid. It's a very faint change but I see it. Anticipation rises in me, and I fight the urge to wiggle.

Calm down, Ember. We have to remain quiet and still. We don't know if someone will exit the cabin. We don't want to be caught, Kai scolds me without moving. He's slightly in front of my bush and I feel an urge to bite his ass in frustration.

I can't help it. I'm new to this, remember? I let out a light huff that disturbs the grass in front of me.

Listen, Ember, we know you're eager to get in there but remain calm. We're here to help but you can't get us caught. Vixie's voice streams through my mind.

I'm trying, guys. I close my eyes and focus on my breathing, trying to chill. All my instincts tell me to bust in and set everything on fire. I can't though because that might harm my sisters.

A growl tries to slip out, but I shift my tongue and bite down on it to prevent it from happening. What the hell is wrong with me right now? The pain seems to help me settle, despite the taste of my own blood spilling down the back of my throat.

The few guards we've found are out. It's not pretty in here but it's safe to come in. Marley's voice startles me and I all but jump up.

Kai growls at me and I stop where I'm at. *Everyone, move in slowly. Proceed with caution.*

Zeke and Ulric move up beside me and place a hand on my shoulders. I roll my eyes and huff as they drop their hands, and we follow Kai out of the brush toward the house. Our footsteps are soundless as if we are trained assassins, which some of our group have been trained to be, as needed.

I watch to the side where Vixie, Cerberus, Leon, and Blaze come out of the trees, looking like a group of badasses. Cerberus motions with his head and their group changes direction to move toward the rear of the house. They must be planning to cover the back in case of attack.

Kai shifts forms at the door and immediately grabs his sword from his back, going on alert. He motions for me to stop, and Zeke and Ulric move closer. He signals for me to change, and I do quickly and pull out my katana.

Kai pushes open the door, and my mates keep a tight ring around me as we move in. The smell hits me as I pass the threshold and gag. I fight the urge to retch as Zeke looks at me with concern.

How the hell did we not smell this out there? I ask the three of them.

Cloaking spell, Ulric responds and Kai shakes his head in agreement.

God, it's terrible, I complain.

Focus, love, Zeke admonishes.

I clamp my teeth together and push forward, looking around as we do. The entryway is sparse, and threadbare carpet covers the floor. The smell of rot and decay hang in the air mixed with the smell of death. It's horrible.

We move into the kitchen and see a sink full of dishes and leftovers all over the bar. How the hell did they eat in here with that stench? Who the hell are these guards?

A small trail of blood catches my eye, leading toward what appears to be some type of mud room, and I spot a couple of guards piled up, lifeless. That must be where the twins deposited them.

Where are you? Kai asks, referring to the twins.

In the basement. Take the hidden door at the bottom of the pantry, Mikai responds.

Kai turns toward what looks to be the pantry and moves forward. He opens the door and I'm impressed with how spacious it is. It's filled with dry goods and a door hangs open in the floor, leading to a flight of stairs.

Dread fills me as the smell of blood and decay gets stronger. What has been happening down there?

Kai leads us in and Ulric and Zeke fall in line behind me as we descend the narrow stairs. My body trembles as I take each step and my magic responds to my emotions, wanting to burst free.

As we reach the bottom of the stairs, I gasp at the horrendous site of cages filled with women. Some have bits of clothing and some are completely naked. Several are leaned up against the bars while others lie on the floor. They have no comfort, and several don't appear to be breathing.

Panic surges through me and I look around wildly. Where are my sisters? Oh my God, are they even alive?

Zeke clamps a hand down on my shoulder, holding me in place as my emotions surge through the bonds with my mates. Sparks fly from my fingers, and I fight the urge to break from their grasp and race forward.

Get it together, Ember. This is not just about your sisters now, Kai growls through our connection.

I glare at him as he turns to face me, and I spy who is in the cages behind him. My eyes widen and my strength surges as I push Zeke off me and sprint to my sisters.

I stare at their bodies on the floor and heat up my hand to melt through the bars. I have to get through to them. I tune everything around me out as I melt through the metal and flames lick up the sides of my body, heating the room. I hear voices around me, but as soon as the iron is warm enough, I burst through it and move to my sisters.

I kneel beside them as tears move down my face, listening to them. *Don't be dead, don't be dead* runs through my head like a mantra chanted during meditation. I lean my head forward and pick up a very faint heartbeat in both of them.

A loud sob escapes me, and I reach out for Zeke. *I need you now. You have to help me save them.*

He's at my side almost instantly. He pulls me back from my sisters gently and kneels beside me. Using a small knife, he slices his palm and lets some of his blood drip into my sisters' mouths by tilting their heads back one at a time.

I watch helplessly as he lays them back on the ground and I realize that cages are opening around us. I glance around and see Ulric and Kai helping others out while Zeke remains with me. I know I need to be helping them, but I am tied to this spot.

A soft moan pulls my attention back to my sisters. Winnie opens her eyes and blinks up at me.

"Em?" Her words are a whisper as she tries to sit up.

"Don't move. Give it a few more minutes. Zeke gave you some of his blood," I say and rest my hand on her arm.

She glances around us. "Are you rescuing us?"

"Of course. You know I wouldn't leave you in the hands of psychos. I'm sorry I didn't get here sooner."

She looks over at Tansy who has yet to open her eyes. "Is she going to be okay? They injected her with something before I passed out. I don't know what it was."

Concern roils in my stomach and nausea rises. What did they put in her?

"She will soon," Zeke says soothingly. "Do you want to try to stand now? We have a safe place to take you."

Winnie nods her head weakly and we help her stand. Once she's up, I have her lean against me as Zeke scoops up Tansy's unconscious form. She's much thinner than she was before. How much weight has she lost?

"Can you shift?" I ask Winnie as we shuffle toward the stairs that lead out of the basement and join the line of women, making their way up.

"I don't know. I can try when we get out of here," Winnies says softly.

"If not, you'll have to hang on to my back. We're going to take you to Cerberus' home. It's not far from here."

Winnie nods in understanding and I can't tell if she's saving her strength for the shift or tired. I think Zeke's blood is the only thing helping her stand and move at this point.

I help her shuffle up the stairs at a slow pace with Zeke keeping close by. As we reach the top, I see Mikai ushering us toward the back door where the rest of our party is. We're almost home free and then we just have to make the trek back to Cerberus' estate.

"We'll work on shifting once we get outside, okay Winnie? Just hang in there." I offer her encouragement and she nods in response.

Joy sparks in my chest that I'll get them out of here. My mother may be dead, but I refuse to lose my sisters too. It won't happen. I'll find a way to keep them here.

As we shuffle through the back door, I see Vixie smiling as she groups the girls together. They hand them small cloaks to wrap around themselves from the bags they brought with them. I'm glad that we decided to bring them even though we weren't sure they would be needed.

I smile at Vixie as I catch her eye and she ushers Blaze to grab two cloaks to take toward Zeke and me. I help Winnie sit on the ground as he approaches and Zeke lays Tansy next to them.

"Will she be okay?" Blaze asks, pointing at Tansy as he hands Winnie a cloak.

"I hope so." I frown and glance up, looking for Kai and Ulric.

Zeke kneels next to Tansy, and I look down at him as he feeds her more blood. "I hope this second dose helps. I don't want to give her too much more."

I lift my brow and meet his gaze as he looks up at me. "What would happen if you gave her more?"

He shrugs. "Well, if she dies, it might turn her or it may not do anything at all. It should keep her stable until we get back but I'm not sure. I've only ever given a second dose to someone capable of turning into a vamp. I don't know how it works on shifters. Hopefully her own healing will kick in."

I stare dumbfounded at his information. "She won't die. I won't let that happen, Zeke. It can't happen. I can't lose anyone else."

Winnie lets out a groan at my words. "What do you mean lose anyone else, Em?"

I turn my gaze to hers and kneel back down. "Now is not the time to have this conversation. We'll talk about it later."

She growls and I can tell her body is recovering slowly now, and her enhanced healing has kicked in. "No, I want to know now. I'm not a child anymore."

"No, Winnie. Now is absolutely not the time. Drop it," I seethe.

"No, tell me now!" She raises her voice, and it seems to echo around us as everyone stops to stare at us.

I drop my gaze, feeling defeated. How can I tell her this? I look up to Zeke, hoping for support but my heart drops as I see a hellhound move out of the trees. I stand to my feet as Zeke whips around and moves in front of my sisters.

The wolf snarls at us and I don't miss how matted his fur is. Two more move out of the trees behind him, followed by a group of brown-winged guards. They all sneer at us as if they've caught a child with his hand in the cookie jar.

I call my magic forth and feel flames burst to life in my hands. I faintly hear our group moving closer, forming a protective circle around the women. My eyes widen as Stole steps from the trees with his sword in hands.

"My, Ember, haven't you assembled a fine group? I'm impressed, dear, really. You have Lucifer's finest hellhounds at your beck and call, but did you know you had a traitor in your midst? She helped us with so many details." Stole twirls his sword and a woman steps out of the shadows.

Charity looks almost unrecognizable. Her hair is cut into a pixie cut and is no longer burgundy but bleached white. Her eyes are black, and she has an eerie smile on her face. What did he do to her?

"Charity has been an excellent assistant. Not only has she helped me but also Greed. You'll be pleased to know that not only have you lost your mother, but your biological father will be gone soon to. Hell will be ours soon," Stole says nonchalantly and my sister gasps behind me.

"Mom is dead?" Winnie asks loudly.

"Now is not the time, Winnie," I say over my shoulder.

Kai steps from our group toward Stole. "We won't let him take Hell and you know that Stole. It will fall to Ember."

Stole chuckles. "Who said you were all leaving here alive. Did you think this small band was all I brought to take you on? I'm not stupid. I do have a request from Charity to have a go at you first, Ember. She took pleasure in killing your mother but said it wasn't enough."

I hear Winnie move forward as if to attack but I whip my hand out faster than she can move and halt her steps. Anger surges through me and flames spread across my body and up my wings.

I stare at Charity. "You killed my mother?"

She smirks. "I did."

Stole laughs and pats Charity on the shoulder. "Oh, this is going to be fun to watch. Go on, Charity darling, have your fun."

Charity walks forward, flames sprouting from her hands. She thinks this will be easy, but I've got a surprise for her.

Feeling like a raging goddess, I step forward and let my powers surge, creating a circle around the women behind me as well as around Charity and me. Like hell anyone will touch my sisters or the people I care about.

I catch surprise spark in Charity's eyes and smile even brighter when I see blue flames swirl into mine. "Bet you didn't expect that did you?" I smile and shift into a fighting stance.

"You're right, I didn't, but I should have expected something new. You've been training with that witch after all." Charity sneers and I watch her begin to shift.

I call forth my hellhound as well and stand facing her with my teeth bared a second later. My fur stands on end as I stare her down. I refuse to let her take the people I love away. I refuse to let her and Stole move forward with their plan. They will not leave this clearing alive.

Charity shifts her weight, preparing to launch herself, but before she can lift a foot off the ground, I charge her. In a blink of an eye, my jaws are around her neck and she's flying over my shoulder as I swing her. She lands in a heap behind me, and I flip around, spinning, sending power into the circle of flames around us.

As I face Charity, Stole's chuckles fill the air behind me. "You are putting up a good effort, Ember. I see that you don't wish us to harm any of the ones you love but you forget hellhounds can move through fire."

A sharp whistle fills the air, and the hellhounds move forward. I don't get a chance to see where they attack first because at that moment, Charity attacks. She took advantage of the distraction and made her rush toward my right shoulder. Her fangs dig into my shoulder and pain fills me like ice.

I can only hope that my mates are keeping my sisters safe and that the rest of our group is taking them out. We are overwhelmed and at a disadvantage. There are more of them than there are of us. I growl in frustration as I continue to face Charity. I need to get her down quick so I can help the others.

With the gashes in my shoulder bleeding, I roar at Charity and fling myself at her. Rage fills me and I let my power engulf me. Flames cover my entire body as I crash into her, pinning her to the ground. She wiggles beneath me, but I refuse to budge as I clamp down on her throat. I let my instincts take over as her blood gushes across my tongue and rip her throat. She convulses under me, but I maintain my hold until I feel her quit breathing.

Spitting out the pieces of her flesh that were stuck in my mouth, I recall my flames and glance around me, figuring out where I need to attack next. Who do I need to help? My heart stops in my chest as I see Zeke and my sister, Winnie, battling side by side, keeping Tansy's body between them. She's still unconscious and I know where I need to go. The three hellhounds trying to take them down won't stand a chance.

I rush at them, throwing flames out as I move and realize they are no longer their normal color but black. I have reached another level of my magic and hellfire hits those around me. Thankfully, it's only enemy beings. How I get lucky with that I'll never know but I dash into the three hellhounds and take them out quick.

Zeke chuckles as I take two down and he takes out the other. Winnie, still in her human form, drops to her knees, thankful that they are backing off. I growl at Zeke and say through our connection, *Step forward. I'm closing her into a safe circle of fire, a safe circle of hellfire.*

Sounds like a plan, love. I'll get out of the way. Don't need to be touching any of that.

I huff and get Winnie's attention. *Make sure you don't touch the flames. You'll be safe. They can't get through these.*

She nods in understanding, and hunkers down next to Tansy, as my flames dance around her, changing from a fiery red color to black. Like hell will I let anything else happen to them. I then reinforce them with the blue magic that stems from the bond Vixie and I have made.

I turn, trying to find my next target and notice Stole still standing in the trees, watching the onslaught. The coward is letting everyone else do his dirty work. As if sensing my gaze, he meets mine and smiles wickedly. He lifts an arm and ushers me to come and get him before he disappears into the trees.

I don't contemplate it for a second before I dart after him, leaving a trail of burning prints behind me. My anger has taken control and this asshole will not live to see another day. Flames lick at the underbrush around me as I bust through the tree line.

I snarl as I hear Stole chuckle ahead of me. He will not get away. I sprint after him for several minutes more before I burst into a clearing. Stole is standing, ready for battle, with his sword as I take him in.

"How about you face me in your winged form, princess? Let's see how your skills have changed. We're far enough away that your mates can't help you now," he sneers.

I blink, realizing my mistake, but shift my form to return to my two legs. "You're an asshole, Stole, and today you die. You're done trying to hurt those I love."

"Oh, that's where you're wrong. I'm not the only one in pursuit of your father's throne."

His statement gives me pause but I push it to the back of my mind. There will always be someone after my father's throne. There will always be some type of threat. With the power he holds, there will always be someone who is unhappy.

I glare at him. "I'll deal with that when the time comes." I pull my sword from the sling on my back, not missing the fact that it's now glowing. I'm amazed but I push it away. I'll figure out this new thing later. I've got to focus on my enemy.

We stare each other down, and I watch as Stole moves slightly to his left. I take a step to my right and so begins the circling. Which one of us will move first? I hold myself back, waiting and watching as Kai has taught me in our training. Stole has many more years of experience on me, and I know he'll anticipate me making the first attack. Newsflash though, I refuse to do it. I'll wait him out if I have to.

"I see you have learned quite a bit since our last meeting. I must admit I'm impressed. I see why your mate has been hailed as one of the best. His training shines through with you. You're waiting. Don't worry though. You won't need to wait any longer." At that, he lunges toward me with inhuman speed, swinging his sword down in an arc.

I rush to bring my own sword up to meet his and they clash together, throwing blue sparks out over me. The power behind his blow causes vibrations to course up my arm but I grit my teeth and push outward, using my power to blast him back. I'm thankful that it pushes him off me, but he returns in a flash.

We dance closely together, trying to get a hit in on the other. I block and parry, focusing to hold my ground. I have no clue how I'm going to take him down. He's stronger and faster than me. There has to be a way though.

He keeps me on the defensive, but even with me moving as fast as I can to block his attacks, he still gets a hit. The hits aren't hard, but I wince as several gashes sting along my arms and bleed. I keep a firm grip on my sword and continue to fight. I scold myself for following him into the trees. Why didn't I signal for someone to follow?

"Give it up, Ember! You're prolonging your fate," Stole says, trying to stab me in the side.

"Never, Stole. I refuse to let you harm anyone else."

In an odd twist, Stole flips his arm and turns his wrist, cutting into my thigh deeply. The pain causes me to buckle, and I pull my sword around to block the blow I know is coming.

Stole is smiling as I look up at him, but a look of surprise crosses his face right before a black blur slams into him.

I land on my knees stunned and look to where a tussle has broken out between Stole and Kai. Kai is in his hellhound form and has managed to get his jaws around Stole's throat. With a snap of Kai's jaws, Stole's throat is gone.

I continue to stare, trying to process what just happened. Is it over?

Kai turns and moves toward me, blood still dripping from his muzzle. He shifts forms mid-stride and drops to his knees next to me. He pulls me close, and I wince as pain from everything courses through me.

"Are you okay?" he asks.

"I will be once my healing kicks in. Thank you for coming." I glance over at Stole's bloodied form as different scenarios of what could have happened play through my head.

"Someone had to. You made a stupid choice in pursuing him alone. I'm glad I was able to get here in time. It seemed I was almost too late."

I nod. "Are the others, okay?"

"Yes, we defeated what was left of his little group and they have started working their way back to Cerberus' estate. There are quite a few injured."

"I guess that's good. Now that we know there aren't any others that will attack us around the cabin, do you think we can send someone out to collect the bodies of the deceased?"

Kai frowns and gets lost in thought for a few minutes. "I believe we can arrange that."

"I think it would be nice to try and figure out who they were to let their families know what happened to them. It gives them closure, you know. At least I hope it will. I would want someone to do that for me if it were my friends or family."

"I understand. It's just a foreign concept for us here. It never happens."

"Well, maybe it needs to become a norm. Hell really needs to get up with the times. Maybe everyone would be less, *I want to kill the other*, if we make changes to things like this."

We trudge through the underbrush and the trees to find our way back to the main trail. We aren't worried about being attacked this time. My heart aches at the death and carnage left behind us but we need to get these women some help.

I watch as Winnie moves on her feet, steadier with each step. I'm happy that she seems to be doing okay, but concern fills me for Tansy. Why isn't she awake yet? The vampire blood should be working. Is it risky to give her more?

As the strange sky begins to lighten, signifying the start of day, Cerberus' estate comes into view. Everyone's mood seems to be lighter with each step closer. The fight is over.

We pass through the gates and an enormous group of people come running toward us. They have blankets, clothes, and warm drinks, that they begin passing out. They even help some of the women by taking them off each other's shoulders. Many have a limp, some are bruised and cut, but in time, healing will kick in, now that they are free of that stinking cabin.

Kai ushers my mates and my sister off to another room as we enter the building. Tansy rests in Ulric's arms. I can tell she's breathing so I know she's alive, and that makes me thankful.

We enter another room, and I notice it has two beds. I assume one is for Winnie and the other for Tansy. We will all need to rest before traveling back to earth and going to my family's home. Maybe more than a day or so, depending on how Tansy is.

Ulric lays her down and I walk to her side. Winnie and I both sit on the bed next to her. I feel her forehead and notice it feels warm and clammy. I look at Zeke, who seems to appear out of nowhere. "Is there anything else you can do?"

"I don't know, love. I can try to give her more blood, but I'm not sure what will happen. I don't know what else is going on."

"She's going to wake up though, right?" I balance on the edge of despair. Something is going on.

Zeke's eyes flicker. "No, love, I'm afraid she's not. Her heart is still struggling and her healing is not kicking in, despite the amount of blood we've already given her. I'm afraid the only option whether I give her more blood or not is to see if she wakes up like me or different. Vampire but not just vampire."

I frown. "If that has to happen, then so be it. At least she'll still be alive."

"True, but she may not want that. What if her existence after the transition is not what she wants?" Zeke is cautious as he asks his daunting question.

I growl in frustration. "We won't know until we try. We have to at least try."

Zeke lets out a sigh. "And if she doesn't want to live after she awakens, will you be the one to kill her?"

My heart stutters in my chest but I square my shoulders. "If I must, then let the heavy burden of that task weigh on my shoulders."

We all remain sitting in silence, staring at Tansy, waiting to see if Zeke will follow my request. Finally, with a heavy sigh, he cuts his hand and presses it to her mouth, pushing her lips apart, so the blood flows in. After a minute of this, he pulls away and props her head up. She goes completely still, no breath, and no heartbeat.

My heart shatters and a sob escapes my lips. This can't be happening! This can't be real!

Winnie sobs next to me and my anger surges through my body. I scream as loud as I can at the universe. How dare it take so many people I care about from this world, from this life I'm living. I get that I'm immortal and I know this will happen but not so soon. She deserved to live a longer life.

Zeke rests his hand on my shoulder. "We'll know if it worked tomorrow, well more so tonight, really. Give it time, Ember. She might come back."

My mates forcefully drag me and my sister from the room, leaving Tansy on the bed. They refuse to leave us in there and carry us to the big suite that I stayed in the night previously. They set both of us down in the heavy bed and I reach for Winnie, pulling her close. We hold each other and cry until we can cry no more. Our bodies are exhausted, and soon sleep drags us down into darkness.

Chapter 24

I pull myself from a deep sleep hours later and find myself still cuddled up with Winnie. She's still sleeping, and I push myself up gently into sitting, doing my best not to disturb her. There's no telling how long it has been since she rested. I slide myself out from beneath the blankets and glance around the room. I wonder where my mates are.

I quietly pad over to the bathroom to clean myself up before letting myself out of the room. I hope Winnie won't be too upset that I've left her alone. She may never want to be alone again after all she's been through.

I head down the hall toward the front of the house, sniffing the air to attempt to locate my mates. I'm not sure what time of day it is but I look out of a window as I pass, and notice night has fallen once again.

I continue, letting my nose guide me, and find them all in a yellow sitting room. They each have a glass of amber liquid and sit with grave looks on their faces. I know they heard me coming. There isn't a reason they didn't unless they're too deep in thought.

I tap on the door. "Hey, any changes?"

They all meet my gaze with a frown. Zeke speaks up, "She's transitioning. It should be done soon. I'm not sure what she'll be like after, Ember. Sometimes when beings wake as a new vampire, they struggle with blood lust, but none that I know of have ever been a shifter."

I move forward and take an open spot next to Ulric who proceeds to wrap me in his arms. "What does that mean?" I feel my anxiety raising its head within.

"It means she may need to go to my kingdom and that she'll have to stay here in Hell," Zeke responds sadly. "At least until we know how things are going to go."

I rub my temples as tension settles there trying to turn into a headache. I can handle this. She's alive at least. "Okay, can Winnie and I at least see her before you take her?"

Cerberus clears his throat. "I'll be taking her, Ember. Zeke will be going with you."

I glance around the room, waiting for someone to explain why Cerberus is doing it and no one does. "Why will you be taking her and not Zeke? He's the prince after all."

Cerberus lets out a sigh. "Turns out she's my mate. I guess there's something about your bloodline that calls to all of us old bastards."

"Hey, who are you calling old, Uncle?" Kai retorts.

My mouth drops open. "Are you kidding me right now?"

Cerberus shakes his head. "Not at all. The opposite actually. I promise that no harm will befall her."

I drop my hands to my lap and stare up at the ceiling as I mutter aloud, "Does the universe have something against me?"

Ulric chuckles softly next to me. "I think it wants to prepare you for anything. You are the heiress of Hell."

"Thanks for the reminder. So how long until she wakes up?"

"It should be anytime now." Zeke shrugs.

"Can I go check?" I slowly stand, pushing Ulric's arms to the side.

"Only if we all go with you," Kai responds.

"That's fair," I say and they lead me from the room.

We slowly walk down the hall toward the room we left Tansy in. I feel my heart race as we near closer and I try to mentally prepare myself for what condition she may now be in on the other side of the door.

As we push into the room, I'm amazed to see that she looks better. Her bruises are gone, but she's not breathing.

"Don't get to close to the bed until after she wakes," Zeke instructs, sticking his arm out and stopping me from stepping forward.

Ulric, Kai, and Cerberus move closer to me as Zeke approaches my sister's still form. He places a hand on her forehead and closes his eyes for a moment. Is he communicating with her? Eventually, her eyes flutter open and she stares at the ceiling. She sits up and looks around the room as if confused. Zeke remains standing next to the bed.

When her gaze lands on me, I can no longer fight the tears threatening to spill down my cheeks. They flow as if a dam has broken somewhere inside of me. Every fear I had on the way here and finding her, releases itself.

"Ember, is it really you?" she asks, pushing from the bed. Her legs buckle and Zeke catches her, eliciting a growl from Cerberus.

"Before you get to close to your sister, Tansy, we need to know if you feel the need to drink blood now. I have a glass of it ready for you, but we have to make sure you won't harm any of us," Zeke says calmly as Tansy blinks in confusion.

"Why would I want blood?" She glances at him and then down at her hands. "Did something happen to me?"

I push forward and move Zeke quickly to the side. Fuck their worry. She's not going to do a thing. I wrap her in a hug against their protests.

"Tansy, I need you to listen closely," I whisper softly. "Sis, you died. Zeke's blood couldn't help you recover. Instead, it caused you to transition into a vampire."

"Oh," she whispers back and begins to tremble. "Is that why I feel weird?"

"Yes, I believe so. We're going to make sure you don't harm anyone. Do you want to try to drink some of the blood Zeke got you?" I pull back and usher for her to return to the bed to sit.

"I guess I could try." She shrugs.

Zeke moves across the room to pick up a large glass. I can smell the coppery scent from where I'm at and it strengthens the closer he moves toward us. I turn away as he hands Tansy the glass and I hear her take a sip. I glance over as she pauses, and I grimace as she begins to chug it like she's dying of thirst.

She takes the cup away from her mouth and licks her lips. "Wow, that was good. Can I have some more?"

"I'll get you some more shortly. I think we need to get you up to speed on things," Zeke responds casually.

"What things?" Tansy looks around astonished.

I let out a heavy sigh. "Well, for one, Mom is dead. The man who had you, had her killed. She's been avenged though."

Tansy sits stunned, staring at me. A sob breaks free of her lips, and she crumples into my arms. I hold her and let my tears flow with hers.

We sit like this for several minutes before Cerberus moves to Tansy's other side and sits down. She whips her head up and looks at him with her nostrils flaring.

Her tears disappear as she asks, "Who are you? Why do you smell like my mate?"

Cerberus chuckles softly but maintains a sad expression. "I'm your mate, little one. I wish we had met under different circumstances, but I wanted you to know."

Tansy leans awkwardly into him and begins sniffing his neck. I groan as she licks his neck and Cerberus lets out a different type of groan.

"I don't think now is the time to do that. We still need to take care of a few other things first." Cerberus lightly pushes Tansy away but keeps his hand resting on her shoulder.

"I'm sorry. I couldn't control myself for a minute." She stares down at her hands.

"That's part of being a new vampire. It'll wear off in time." Zeke chuckles. "I'll tell you now that you're not too distracted, Tansy, Cerberus will be taking you to my kingdom for a time until you can handle your new abilities."

"Why? They can't be much different from what I had before, can they?" She crosses her arms defiantly across her chest, making me chuckle. We share a stubborn streak.

"Well, hopefully, but we've never had a shifter transition to a vampire before so there may be some things we didn't expect." Zeke leans against a wall across the room from us.

"We'll be leaving as soon as your sister rises. I'm sure you want to see her before we go," Cerberus chimes in. Kai and Ulric remain quiet.

"Is she okay?" Tansy looks at me.

"Winnie seems okay so far. Emotionally, I'm not sure. I don't know what you two went through." I drop my arms onto my lap.

Tansy zones out for a few minutes before she responds to my words. "A lot. We went through a lot."

"Do you want to talk about it?" I ask concerned.

Tansy shakes her head. "When I'm ready, we'll talk. Give me time, sis."

I nod and turn to the door as it pushes open. A sleepy-eyed Winnie blinks at us for a second before launching across the room and tackling us into a bear hug on the bed. Tears flow again. After we've recovered enough, and the guys are assured that Tansy won't do any harm to her sisters, they leave us alone.

We cry and catch up for hours, pausing only to eat some of the food the guys bring us. Well, more blood for Tansy. Eventually, we fall into an exhausted heap across the bed, each of us knowing that upon waking, we'll all be leaving—Tansy to Zeke's kingdom and Winnie and I to earth.

When we wake, we all drag ourselves out of the bed and dress. We don't have much time left together so we take as long as we can. All our worlds are about to change permanently once we leave.

A few hours later, we say our goodbyes, standing before a portal Cerberus guided us to. Kai insists on leading us through, ever the general. I roll my eyes but let him lead. I'm dreading the next few days.

I hug Tansy tightly before releasing her. Cerberus reassures me that he'll take care of her, and I let her go. With a smile, I grab Ulric's hand as he stands before the misty portal. Giving Tansy one last look, I take a deep breath, and step through the mist with my mates and sister, Winnie. We have a long way to go before we get back to my pack in Oklahoma.

Chapter 25

Popping out of the portal, I glance around, trying to figure out where we are.

"This is not New Orleans." I look at Kai who is scratching his head in confusion.

"No, it's not. I'm not sure what happened. We're in Taos, New Mexico." He crosses his arms and looks over at Zeke and Ulric.

Zeke shrugs. "Don't look at us. You were the first to enter. It was up to you to pick the destination. You know how it works."

Ulric rolls his eyes and grunts. "Let's just figure out how to get to Ember's pack."

Kai glances at me, "if I remember correctly, there is a small organic grocery store not far from here. A lesser demon used to run it and keep an eye on this portal for us. She should still be there. We can see if she has something for us to use to get to Oklahoma."

Ulric tilts his head. "Is someone watching all the gates?"

Kai nods. "They're supposed to be, yes."

Ulric looks concerned. "The one we used in Alaska didn't have a guardian."

Zeke chuckles. "That's because the gate there is under the water. Not an easy one to watch."

Kai frowns. "There should have been someone there though. We'll have to fix that."

"Can we focus please?" I glance at my three mates, pausing their conversation. "We need to get a move on. Things to do, you know?"

"Right, Ember, we just have to go into town." Kai motions for us to follow and we start off at a steady pace.

We enter a small town three hours later and find the grocery store Kai mentioned. A slim woman with bright pink hair recognizes us instantly and wordlessly motions for us to follow her. She leads us through her small store to a back door.

As we push through, I expect to find a basement, but instead it opens up into a small garage. She finally speaks after closing the door behind us.

"I'm Nadia. I've been waiting for someone to use the portal closest to me for years. My gate isn't used as much now." She steps forward and removes a large tarp off a black suburban. "This will get you to wherever you need to go. I won't ask for details, that's not my job. Don't worry about returning it. I'll send a message in to have a new one purchased. Just hit the garage door opener when you're ready to leave. There is a cloaking spell over this part of the building, and it will hold on to the car until it touches the main road."

She smiles, bows, and quickly returns to the shop.

I stare, gaping at how quickly she left. "Is that normal?"

Kai laughs. "Yes, normally those stationed at the gates don't interact at all. Let's get in. We have some traveling to do."

"Why can't we travel like we did in Hell?" I ask curiously and glance at my sister. She seems like she could keep pace with us all now.

Ulric chuckles deeply. "We would be too suspicious, love. We need to stay under the radar."

I nod. "Right, okay. Let's get moving."

§

Two tiring days later, we pull up to my family home. We're all travel weary but thankful that the suburban was comfortable as we traveled. We did make a stop halfway to rest. It seems that the battle with Stole and his group took more out of us than we realized.

As we sit parked in the drive, Winnie and I stare out at our house while the guys stretch beside the car. There is no turning back from it now and going in will hit me and her both hard. Mom will not be there.

"We can do this," I say over my shoulder from the passenger seat. "We have to, Winnie. Dad needs us, and Mom would want us to all to be together."

I push open my door and step out of the car. I hear Winnie get out behind me and take a deep calming breath. As she moves to my side, I take her hand and we move toward the house together. I let everything around me fall away as I reach the steps and take them slowly. Winnie and I take a deep breath before we push into the house.

Dad rounds the corner from the kitchen with a look of death that changes to surprise instantly upon seeing us. He stops in his tracks as tears begin to fall freely from his eyes. "Tansy, is she?"

I shake my head. "She's alive. She's no longer a shifter though. She's a vampire. She has to go spend time in the vampire kingdom before she can come here."

He sinks to the floor and drops his head into his hands and begins to sob. I rush forward, Winnie at my side, and we kneel next to Dad.

"She's okay, Dad. We're all okay. We're home." I wrap my arms around him.

"But your mother," he gasps out.

"We know, Dad. We know." Winnie says softly.

We remain in a huddle on the floor for at least an hour before Corey, Adam, and Seth arrive. They convince us to move to the living room while Corey gets us drinks. I blink at everyone wordlessly, fighting to get my emotions under control as I sit on the couch, watching my mates pick up the messy house around us. It isn't bad and I assume Seth has been in and out helping, but it's also not the same.

Eventually, with several bags of chips laid out on the table and every-one holding some type of drink, Adam clears his throat.

"I know that a lot has happened, Ember, but the council will be here tomorrow. They want to speak with every member of the pack. That still includes you despite things." He glances around the room. "Can you han-dle that?"

I sip at the pop in my hands for a moment, mulling it over. We came to help. "Yes. I'll do what is needed but I think they should know who I really am. I think it's time to establish that there is more involved here."

Corey adds, "I agree. I think it'll help with flushing out those who seek only evil in this pack."

"You realize this may start a war within your pack, right?" Zeke throws his question out, causing us to all pause.

"I think we had some idea that it would happen anyway. Corey and I have been gathering allies," Adam says confidently.

"Do we need to be prepared to fight tomorrow?" Kai asks concerned. "I sent the rest of our group to finish a task, but I'm sure we can send word to them and have them here quickly."

"Hopefully not." Adam frowns. "I think we need to wait it out and see."

"Okay, but not too long, Adam. I don't want your father to pull one over on us. He's been doing it for too long."

Adam rubs his forehead. "I know but we can't just throw him in a prison. He's got a witch working with him."

"Fuck, I forgot about her." I groan. "Kai, we need to get Vixie here. I may need her to help me with this witch."

"We can do that. Let's call Lucifer through the compact." He nods toward my bag.

I pull my bag up into my lap from the floor and dig around for the compact mirror. I find it at the very bottom and thankfully it's not broken. I open it and quickly move through the process of calling the king of Hell. Instead of his face showing up, Minerva appears.

"Hi, Minerva, is Lucifer around?" I ask, noticing her frown.

"Dear, your father has been poisoned. I'm working on him now but it's not good. He has a long road ahead of him to pull out of it."

I stare at her stunned. "How can he be poisoned? I thought only those with specific blood could harm the original fallen?"

"Well, I'm afraid that is what has happened. We discovered the problem after the ball when you were gone. He's stable but we're having to push fluid through his system frequently to fight the toxins. I'm hoping to have it stopped within two weeks, but only time will tell." Minerva looks down as if checking something before looking back at the mirror.

"How soon do I need to come back?" I ask worried.

"You are fine right now. I'll reach out to you if you need to come back sooner. Did you call for something in particular?" She lifts a brow.

"Yes, sorry, I did. I need you to send a message to Vixie to head this way. Our witchy friend may be involved with attacks on the pack here."

"That bitch." I stare, astonished at Minerva's language. "I'll deliver the message and send her with some extra potions. If you two must face her, you're going to have your hands full. Do you have another witch that could aid you or maybe more?"

I pause and think back to our trip south. "Maybe? I can ask at least one."

"Get any extra witch help you can if you must face her there. It would be different if you were to encounter her in Hell. I could help you more easily, but there, you are on your own. I'll send some more books to aid you as well." Minerva frowns. "I must go, dear. I'll have her on her way today."

"Thanks, Minerva. Alert me if there are any changes," I say and we end the conversation.

I glance up to see concerned faces all around. Kai appears tense and like he is forcefully holding himself back from darting out the door to return to Hell.

"He's going to be okay. Minerva is tending to him," I say to the room, eyeing Kai specifically.

"I should be there protecting him," he says in a low tone.

"He was poisoned when we were all there," I respond. "Minerva is tending to him. We will be back soon."

He sighs loudly. "You're right. I have a lot of guilt though. What do we need to do here?"

I frown and look over at Adam who appears worried. He looks at Corey before meeting my gaze. "I think the only thing we can do right now is wait."

To be continued in Living Flames...

Afterword

As Ember's story continues, I sincerely hope you too will continue along with her. Thank you for picking up this second installment in my Ember series. Without you the reader, this book wouldn't have come to fruition. I would love to hear your thoughts on the story and for you to hang out with me on my social media. Please leave a review where you purchased your copy from to help me grow my audience. Check out more of my work and keep up with what's going on with my book world by checking my website and signing up for my newsletter. www.thechaptergoddess.com

For more of my books checkout my bookstore on my website.

Acknowledgements

I would like to thank all of those who put time in to helping me complete this book. Joe Compton, Ron Lahr, both with Go Indie Now, Venessa Giunta with The Writing Tribe, Sean Hillman with The Night Owls writing group within The Writing Tribe, my husband and my son, my family and so many more. Huge thanks to the readers, beta readers, and ARC readers as well. So many people helped make this book dream come true.

A special thanks to my dedicated editor Ms. K Edits and to the Cover artist Arash Jahani. You two really made the book come to life.

About the Author

Madilynn Dale is an author based out of Oklahoma City, Oklahoma, U.S. She writes fantasy, romance, and paranormal pieces primarily. She spends most of her day with her son, tending to her pets, and writing.

Madilynn holds degrees in several areas. She has a bachelor's degree in Kinesiology from Southern Nazarene University, located in Oklahoma. She also has an Associates of Science degree in Physical Therapy Assistant Sciences from Oklahoma City Community College. She is licensed as a Physical Therapy Assistant in Oklahoma and works as a PRN therapist.

Madilynn has enjoyed reading various forms of fiction and the occasional non-fiction story since she began reading as a young girl. Writing seemed to be another piece of this addiction to books, and she embraced it after becoming a mother. Writing is now a piece of her soul to be bared to the world.

Madilynn's hobbies, when not writing, include reading, baking, crafting, hiking, and horseback riding. She loves to travel and explore. One day she hopes to expand her travels and see the world, but in the meantime, you will find her working on her next novel. She will most likely have coffee and some form of chocolate with her as she writes.